COWBOYS & SUNRISES

A STARLIGHT SWEET ROMANCE

JACQUELINE WINTERS

Editor: EJ Runyon, Bridge to Story

Copy Editor: Brenda Letendre, Write Girl Editing Services

Cover Design: Victorine Lieske

Proofreading: Michelle Josette, www.mjbookeditor.com

CHAPTER 1

J illian

Jillian Harper dangled a treat below her outstretched camera. "Milo! Hey, Milo!" She wiggled the bone-shaped morsel, hopeful to catch the natural light in her studio-converted rancher's cabin. But her golden retriever did little more than blink toward the front window and let out a heavy sigh. "You don't want your treat?"

Nothing.

"You know he doesn't like the camera." Brantley dismounted the ladder, drill in hand. The bracket that held up her starry backdrop had been pulling its way out of her wall for almost a week. She was about as handy as a garter snake and had been forced to call on the help of the ranch's handyman to secure it.

"He'll go for it." She ignored Brantley's disbelieving stare, determined to coax Milo to sport the goofy, adorable grin he'd worn only minutes before. "Eventually."

Brantley rubbed his hand along the back of his neck and over the top of his head, tousling his dusty blond hair. "Maybe you need better treats."

"But he likes these treats." She studied her disinterested dog and pondered Milo's sudden lethargy. They'd gone for a moderate three-mile walk along dirt trails on the outskirts of the ranch this morning. But it was nothing he wasn't used to if the weather cooperated. "You don't think he's sick, do you? Maybe I should take him to the vet."

Brantley folded the ladder and carried it to the front door, careful to avoid dragging it along the hardwood floors. It didn't matter anyway. They'd been scratched and beaten up from years of ranch hands living in the house. "I don't think he's sick, Jilly. I think he doesn't like you taking his picture."

"But how does he know?"

"You take pictures of him all the time." Brantley grabbed his cowboy hat off the coat rack near the front door to set it on his head. "You really think he hasn't figured out what you're up to?"

"But his eyes look extra droopy today. I don't think that's normal. I'm calling—"

"Milo, you want pizza?"

The dog's head popped up and snapped toward Brantley, who now stood in the open doorway sporting a crooked smile. Life had returned to the dog's sleepy eyes.

"See?" He lifted the folded ladder over the threshold and reached for the door handle from the front porch. A gentle summer breeze rustled the few papers on her desk. "You have to know what motivates him."

"You promised him something you don't have," she shot back. "You planning to bring a pizza soon?" The ranch and all of its buildings were a little past the pizza delivery area. No amount of begging had changed that in the last year since Jillian set up her photography shop on her best friend's family ranch.

"Looks like he's looking at you now." Brantley briskly closed the door.

"Crap." She'd said *pizza* last. She pushed up off her knees, lifting the camera strap over her head. Milo wore wide, excited eyes at the promise of his favorite handout.

"Way to play your hand, Milo."

The golden retriever wagged his tail with vigor. He proceeded to stretch in long, exaggerated motions before he trotted over to her and licked her hand. She wrapped her arms around his neck and hugged him hard for a moment. "I have to run into town soon. We'll pick up *something* then."

She dropped into her seat behind a dinky desk. The worn cedar surface was swallowed almost completely by a computer monitor. She prepared to edit photos from a house shoot she'd done yesterday as Milo curled up on his dog bed. As much as she longed to be the most sought-after event photographer, real estate shoots and the occasional professional headshot were keeping the lights on.

Her eye caught the shimmer of her current blue background with its light coating of silver. She smiled. She was fortunate there was someone like Brantley to help her. Fortunate that her best friend let her rent this former rancher's cabin as both studio and home in exchange for occasional chores and the cost of utilities. The cabin wasn't much of a studio, but it was hers.

She lost herself in editing photos for the three-bedroom ranch until her front door swung open.

"Are you actually working?" her best friend Holly Maxwell teased. Milo jumped up from his slumber to greet the ranch manager, his head poking around her legs, hopeful. "Sorry, bud, your brother's at home."

Though their dogs were siblings from the same litter, Holly rarely brought her own to the studio. Where Milo was mellow, Holly's dog was rambunctious and tended to knock everything over with his overeager tail. Including, on occasion, small children.

"I *do* work sometimes, you know." Jillian smiled

at her best friend, saving her progress on the computer. It was a joke between them because if there was one thing she did a lot of, it was work. She hoped to someday only do things related to running a successful photography studio. But for now, she took photos where she could and picked up odd shifts at the local diner.

Holly dropped into a plush chair—the only cushioned seat in the whole cabin—and asked, "What are you working on?"

"House shoot." With a forced smile, she tried to keep the glumness out of her tone, but if the inquisitive look on Holly's face was any indication, she had failed. "That blue house off Danberry Drive."

"The Jeffersons are selling?"

She shrugged. "Sounds like they're packing up and moving to Arizona."

Holly crossed her legs, then uncrossed them. "Got a lot of these house shoots lately."

Yes, she did. "They pay decent." She didn't look up from her monitor. "Don't take much time."

"But you hate it."

She could feel Holly's eyes burning a hole into the back of her computer monitor. "Just . . . not exactly what I expected, you know? I want to shoot special occasions. Capture memories and emotions. Houses are so . . ."

"Inanimate?" Holly offered.

"Precisely."

"What've you been doing lately to grow your business?" It was a question Holly asked at least a couple of times a month. A question Holly's grandpa asked when teaching her to run the ranch.

"I've been scouting local wedding and anniversary announcements online. Emailing them offers to shoot the events." She left out the part that no one had taken her up on said offers. They'd either already booked a photographer or never responded.

"You've got to think outside the box. Think bigger picture."

"Tomorrow night, I'm teaching a class on how to take pictures with smartphones."

"That's better. Definitely something different."

Milo barked once, tail wagging from his perch at the front window. "Lunch has arrived," Holly announced.

"Lunch?"

"Yeah, I had Bobby run some errands in town. Pick up food for everyone." Holly opened the door wide enough to snatch a pizza box from whomever stood on the porch and then slam it closed again, lest Milo escape. "Figured you could use a pizza."

Milo ran circles around them both until they were seated at the small table pushed up against a wall in the back corner. Four chairs sat around it. She used the table for many purposes: lunch, consults with clients, and sometimes playing solitaire when things were slow.

"What kind?" she asked.

"Chicken, bacon, ranch."

Brantley's favorite, if she recalled correctly. No doubt he'd be by later to make sure the bracket held. Now she could thank him with pizza, because the man refused to be paid for anything he fixed. She assessed Holly's expression, but the woman gave away nothing when it came to her cousin or her motives. "Good call."

Once the box lid popped opened, Milo plopped a seat right at the edge of the table—one that was just the right height for his line of sight—and waited. "Or lucky coincidence?" she asked.

"You have any napkins?" Holly avoided the question.

Much to her dog's dismay, she pushed back from her chair and went in search of paper towels. She was sure a roll was stashed in her bottom desk drawer, among a myriad of other random things.

In the middle of riffling through her drawer, the flashing display of her phone resting next to her keyboard caught her eye. Incoming call. Her dad. She groaned. It was probably about his wedding. One she RSVP'd no to last week. "Better rip off the Band-Aid," she muttered, swiping the answer button before Holly could ask what she meant. She had ignored the last three calls. "Hey, Dad."

Holly's eyes widened with curiosity. She waved

the thin roll of paper towels at her friend so she'd stay at the table.

"Sweet Pea, is now an okay time? I know you're busy." The way her dad said that, as though he actually believed she was swamped, sent a twinge of guilt through her. She may have exaggerated her schedule a tad. She'd like to blame the wedding she was avoiding, but truth be told, she had been embellishing the details of her life for a while. Her dad hadn't been to Starlight in almost a decade to witness the inconsistencies in her stories.

"I'm having a bite of lunch." The aroma of freshly baked pizza traveled the length of the room, taunting her. But prolonging this conversation would only put her on edge the rest of the day. "What's up?"

"Got your RSVP. You're sure you can't make it?"

"I'm sorry, Dad. There's a big wedding in town that weekend. They've had me booked for weeks." There *was* a wedding in town that same weekend. That detail was true. But they'd hired her competitor from Buffalo Springs, the next town over, to take the photos.

"I was afraid of that." The disappointment in his voice nearly broke her, made her want to give in. If only she liked Stella, the woman Dad was planning to marry. But of course, she couldn't tell him she couldn't handle her future stepmonster's passive-aggressive comments on the weekend of their wedding.

Awkwardness hung in the air as she searched for soothing words. Anything to ease the sting of his only daughter forfeiting his second wedding. But none came.

"It's not the money, is it? I offered to cover your ticket to Cancun—"

"It's not the money, Dad." Though it kind of was. She could buy all sorts of things her studio needed for the cost of a plane ticket to Mexico's peninsula.

Her dad cleared his throat. "Well then, we came up with plan B."

"Plan B?"

"We know you're a very busy woman, running your own photography studio. Booked out for months. But what if we came to you? Got married in Starlight?"

Panic settled in. "What? Dad, you don't even like it here." He only moved to Starlight all those years ago to fulfill some dream about being a cowboy. But when that dream didn't pan out quite the way he planned, he packed his bags and left her and Mom behind when Jillian was only fifteen.

"There was a time I really enjoyed living there." She almost believed him when he said that. "I've been showing Stella the pictures you send. We agree that if this is what we need to do to include you, it's what we're going to do."

For once, she was speechless. "Starlight, huh?"

"Still have my cowboy hat."

She brought her hand to her forehead, covering her eyes as if that alone could erase the embarrassing image burned into memory. "Please don't bring that."

"Stella thinks it's quite dreamy."

She would. "Dad, please stop." Pizza no longer sounded appetizing. Nothing did. She wondered how hard it would be to keep her dad and future stepmonster away from her pitiful excuse for a photography studio for a couple of days. Surely she could claim it was being painted or renovated. "But wouldn't you have to postpone the wedding? I wouldn't want you to do that."

"Opposite, actually. That's why we're considering it." There was some shuffling on the other end of the phone, some mumbling that sounded partially female, and then, "You're on speaker, Sweet Pea. Stella's here too."

"Jill, darling! How are you?"

"It's Jillian." She hated being called Jill. Hated it even more when her future stepmom addressed her by that. "So, Starlight, really? Stella, it's a pretty small town. Rugged. We don't have an airport. No mall. Or sushi." There. That should do the trick. The little Wyoming town lacked all of Stella's favorite things.

"Oh, that's no bother. Our caterer's willing to make whatever we want, sushi included. And he's willing to travel. Plus, we've been watching that renovation show on TV. Starlight looks positively dreamy!"

She cringed, considering the money it would cost for a caterer and crew to travel halfway across the country. Then the specialty food . . . Her dad could no doubt afford whatever Stella dreamed up, and that had always worried her more than anything with the women he'd dated since divorcing Mom. What if it didn't work out? She tried again, "It sounds like an awful lot of trouble. And then to have to reschedule everything—"

"Oh, Jill, it's no trouble at all!" Stella chimed, sounding a little *too* excited. "In fact, we already made some calls. Everything we want is open next weekend."

She felt thankful she hadn't been eating a slice of pizza. She would've choked. "*Next* weekend?"

Holly dropped her slice on her plate and scooted out of her chair to join her at her desk.

"You said it was the first weekend you had free in a long time, right?" Dad asked.

Crap. She had said that in a text a few days ago, hoping to prolong a conversation about the wedding as long as possible. "Yep."

Stella trilled, "How perfect is that?"

"What about your guests? Surely they can't all make it on such short notice? And the venue change—"

"The important ones will be there," Stella said, nonchalant. "And the venue's no matter. They were willing to spring for Cancun, after all. The airline is more than willing to accommodate. My brother works for them, you know."

She wanted to argue another angle, but she was out of polite objections.

"What do you say?" Dad asked. "We really want you to be part of the wedding, Sweet Pea. It would mean the world to us. And this way, we don't have to inconvenience you."

"Next weekend?"

"Yes!" Stella answered instantly.

"Did you want me to take the pictures?" She thought she might be able to handle a job that at least gave her an excuse to disconnect a little. It would allow her to play the part of successful photographer. She really did love shooting weddings. They gave her the best opportunity to circulate in the background and snap some of the most authentic moments. She'd only had two so far, but Dad and Stella didn't need to know about her lack of experience.

"Oh, we don't want you to worry about working," Dad said.

"Of course we don't," Stella added. "We booked a professional. Plane ticket purchased and everything."

Holly's eyes widened with Jillian's deeply inhaled breath. She probably overheard that part. Or maybe it was the roll of paper towels crushed in her fist that caused the alarm.

"The best part is that new hotel. Did we mention? They even have a honeymoon suite!" Stella kept right on talking as if her words weren't making Jillian's stomach queasy. "Oh, I put you down for a plus one. Your daddy and I are so excited to meet that hunky man you talk about so much!"

Holly's face went as white as Jillian felt. She definitely heard that part. In this whole crazy conversation, she had forgotten about the man she made up. The one who didn't exist. She'd been single since she gave Jason's ring back a year ago. But her dad didn't know that.

"I always forget his name," her dad said.

"Uh—"

"You two are still together, right?" Stella jumped in. "My nephew Chad is coming. I could always put him down as your plus one. He's that super successful photographer from Philadelphia. You remember him, don't you?"

Her fingers curled around the phone. Before she could risk crushing what the phone company probably considered an indestructible phone, she spit out, "I have a plus one. Everything is great. He'll be there."

Holly's eyes widened at that. Her friend's expression begged her to put the conversation on speakerphone. But the echo in the studio was too annoying to do that, and she didn't want to be on the line any longer than necessary.

"Great!" Dad boomed. "Can't wait to finally meet this young man."

"What's his name?" Stella asked.

Holly sprinted to the front door and shook it open enough to jingle the bells. "Oh! Got to go," she said, relieved for the out. "My next clients just came in. Send me your itinerary, okay, so I know when to expect you. Love you. Bye." She ended the call and dropped the cell with a clatter.

"Wow, that sounded intense!" Holly swiped the paper towels—now sporting a skinny middle from where she had crushed the roll—and pulled her arm toward the table. "Did you really just tell them you're bringing your *boyfriend?*"

Milo sat patiently, eyes bouncing from the pizza to his owner. He let out a tiny whine, letting her know how much he felt excluded from their lunch plans.

She fell into a chair and let out a sigh. "Yes." She covered her face with her hands. "That woman—she makes me so crazy!" She wasn't hungry anymore, but she pulled a slice onto her paper plate so she could pick at the crust to share with Milo. "That's not even the worst part."

Holly's eyes lent sympathy. "What exactly have you told your dad?"

A pitiful laugh escaped her throat. "That I'm the

most in-demand photographer for a hundred miles. That I have a nice studio and am thinking about expanding."

"What about this boyfriend part?"

"They don't know I broke up with Jason. I never had a chance to tell them about the engagement, but I also failed to mention we aren't together anymore. The last time I visited, Stella tried so hard to set me up with her irritating nephew, that I went on and on about my *boyfriend* in hopes she'd stop."

"You broke up a year ago."

She didn't realize she'd been tearing at her pizza crust so intently until she looked down to find a dozen tiny morsels. Milo might be disappointed that his usually large portion size had shrunk. "What am I going to do?"

"How long will they be in town? Probably a few days, right?"

She lobbed a piece of crust to Milo, who, despite her poor toss and its tiny size, caught it midair. "Yeah."

"Surely we can figure out someone who'd go along with playing your boyfriend for a couple of days. Didn't sound like they even remembered his name." A mischievous twinkle danced in Holly's eyes. "I think I have an idea."

CHAPTER 2

*B*rantley

Brantley West rolled his Jeep to a stop near the tiny farm's quaint red barn, hardly a quarter mile from the city limits of Starlight. A beautiful caramel-colored mustang with a reddish black mane and stunning light blue eyes trotted to the fence in greeting.

"Hey there, Buttercup." He reached in his pocket for her favorite McIntosh apple and held it out in offering. Once she scooped it up, he ran his hand along her smooth neck. Seemed she'd been brushed this morning. He smiled, hoping today had been a good day for his great aunt Edie.

He spent most of his time at the family ranch,

doing a little bit of everything from ranching chores to handyman tasks. But a couple of times a week, he carved out time to check on Edie and take care of her horse.

"Beautiful day, isn't it?" Edie stood on the cozy covered front porch, a light shawl wrapped around her tiny frame like a blanket. The fence of the horse pasture butted up to the side of the attached garage. Everything about this little farm was cozy, the way Edie had always preferred it.

"I love this time of year," she said, as a promising smile crossed her face. Her white hair was curled and styled; another good sign. "Everything is green and lush. The sun warms the skin."

"Makes a person want to sit outside on a porch swing all day," he added.

He was happy to see her in such positive spirits. Some days, Edie seemed content. Happy even. Others, she sobbed through their entire visit. Those days were hard for both of them. Edie was still missing her husband, gone two years now. One year longer than his brother. He wasn't much good at helping her cope. Hadn't really figured it out for himself.

"How are things at the ranch?" She always asked that question. She'd spent summers there as a kid, but now only made it by for the occasional holiday.

"Good as always." He filled her in about the horses, how the herd looked, and how great his cousin Holly was doing running the ranch now with her grandpa's advisement. "You should come out one day." He said that each time, too.

"Maybe."

"I think it'll be a great day for a ride." He left Buttercup and hopped up the two steps to the front porch to wrap his tiny great aunt in a hug. "A few clouds in the sky. Perfect." He followed her inside so they could enjoy their mutual cups of coffee before he took Buttercup for some exercise.

"How's your mom?" Edie asked once he took a seat in her kitchen. The round table was small and snug in this little space but it held a surprising amount of food when it needed to.

He tensed a bit at the question that wasn't so typical. His mom had packed her bags, her house, her life, the week after Paul's memorial service and fled town. They hadn't spoken much in the last year. "Okay, I think."

"You need to give her a call." Edie slid a cup of steaming coffee and a spoon across the table toward him, along with his favorite hazelnut creamer. She kept it stocked ever since he finished his time in the Army and moved back home. Hard to believe that life was more than a year and a half behind him now.

He scooted his chair closer to the table and rested his elbows on its wood surface. "I'll do that soon."

Edie leveled him with a stern gaze.

He covered one of her hands with his own, meeting her eyes. "I promise." He ignored the tremor that came with the reality of the vow he just made. He never lied to Edie, never would.

She sipped her coffee and the two sat in companionable silence for a bit. It was one of the things he appreciated most about his great aunt. They could sit at the table, drink their coffee, and not say a word. A newspaper sat folded beside the arm she rested on the table, but she wouldn't read it until he left.

"Anything you need me to do before I head back to the ranch?" he asked as he emptied his cup. He'd need to mow the lawn the next time he came by, but it still looked presentable.

"Got a kitchen cabinet door that's a little loose." Edie carried both cups to the sink and rinsed them out. "Can't think of anything else."

"Easy enough." He pushed out of his chair. "Better get Buttercup her exercise." He gave Edie a quick kiss on her cheek, then slipped out the front door.

He was happy to see the barn was still in good order after that windy storm they had a couple of nights ago. He wasn't sure how well the roof would hold, but aside from a stray that had blown to the ground, it appeared to have the rest of its shingles. He picked up the bit of roofing and took it into the barn. Something he could fix during his next visit.

Which reminded him he needed to swing by

Jillian's studio to make sure that bracket was still holding. He saddled Buttercup and slipped on his worn Stetson to keep the sun at bay, then led the horse out of her pasture and toward the trails that ran along the edge of the property.

Buttercup had been a member of the family for nearly fifteen years. Edie often regaled him with stories of her and her husband, Frank, taking long rides to watch the sunset when they were both younger and a bit more agile.

But Edie was no longer brave enough to ride Buttercup on her own; Frank had always seen to her care and exercise. "I can't afford to fall off," she said the last time it came up. "Not at this age. One broken hip, and that's it for me. But I can't bear to part with Buttercup. She's family."

Once Frank passed, Holly stopped over a couple of times a week until Brantley moved back home and could do it himself.

At the trailhead, he hesitated. He'd been taking Buttercup down the trail to the west now for over a year. Surely the mare was tired of the same trail, as it offered little opportunity for variety. It was scenic, but not like the one to the east.

Buttercup took a couple of steps to the eastern trail, but didn't put up much fuss when Brantley redirected her west. "Sorry, girl."

The smoother trail did offer the horse the opportunity to pick up speed, which she did seem to enjoy in small bursts. Within minutes, they'd both forgotten the other trail, and that was fine with him.

"How's Miss Edie been doing, Buttercup?" he asked when the cozy farmhouse was but a speck behind them. "She seems good today."

Buttercup let out a soft neigh but offered nothing more on the subject.

Though Edie didn't ride, she loved Buttercup very much. With the pasture so close to the house, Brantley often caught her outside, nose to nose with Buttercup, stroking her neck. *I don't know what I would do without you, Brantley. If you weren't here to take care of Buttercup, I'd have to give her up.* That little reminder always made him feel guilty for leaving in the first place. He'd been in the Army, stationed in Alaska with six months left in service when his great uncle Frank passed away.

Slowing Buttercup from a gallop to a slow trot for a sharp turn up ahead, Brantley wished as he did every time he hit this scenic spot with its rolling hills that he wasn't riding alone. He imagined Jillian riding along, enjoying the views and serenity with him.

He wondered what it would take to get her back on a horse again. She helped with the horse chores a couple of days a week on the ranch, and was good with the horses as long as she was on the ground. It was only that his cousin Holly had told him about her fall that he knew at all. But Jillian didn't know that.

And just like that, he felt twisted and torn inside.

He'd been in love with Jillian longer than he could remember. Longer than any sane man would dare pine after a woman. She'd never once given him a reason to hope she saw him as more than a friend, and so often she'd been dating someone else. There'd been a time, a few months after her broken engagement, that he thought maybe . . . But then the news arrived home about Paul, and everything in his world went sideways.

They were friends, and he wasn't willing to jeopardize what they'd formed over a mushy confession that could go south very quickly. It was better to have her in his life this way than to not have her at all.

"It's for the best, Buttercup."

He had received more than a few dating offers since moving back to Starlight, but none of them ever held a candle to Jillian Harper. He could still remember the first day she started working on the ranch as a teenager looking for extra spending money. Her auburn hair was shorter then, hardly brushed her shoulders. These days, she wore it longer, usually up in a messy bun.

"I think right here is the perfect spot for a break," he said, halting Buttercup. He fed her another apple, then went to find a spot atop a wide smooth rock firmly wedged into the ground. Modest mountains stood in the background beyond green rolling hills illuminated by the sun while the rest of the sky was overcast.

He imagined if Jillian were here now, her camera would be out and aimed at the picturesque moment. He'd only seen a few of her landscape photos, as she seemed to favor people and events. But there was no doubt in his mind that she had a gift, much like Paul.

At the constriction of his throat, he forced himself to take a deep breath. He'd never been as close to his older brother as he wanted, not even after joining the Army to follow in his footsteps and hopefully make him proud. It was a concept his mom had never understood or supported.

He pulled his phone from his pocket, curious whether there might be a signal this far out. It would be better to call his mom now and get it over with so he could at least tell Edie he'd done it. The conversation, if there even was one, wouldn't be pleasant. Their relationship had been strained at best since the day he boarded the plane for basic training, now almost six years ago. After Paul's passing, it'd only gotten worse.

With three out of four bars, he had no excuse. His finger hovered over the call button, trembling ever so slightly. It was the wind, he told himself. Buttercup whinnied from behind. "She might not even answer."

Before he could commit to the call, a notification popped up on his screen.

Jilly.

He feared his heart would always pound like cannon fire when he saw her name on his screen.

Jilly: Can you stop by the studio? Need a small favor :)
Brantley: Sure. Be by in an hour.
Jilly: Thanks a mil!

He decided he could make the call later. He never promised Edie he would do it today, only soon. He dropped his phone back in his shirt pocket, unable to fight off the smile that crept across his lips. At least now he wouldn't have to make some lame excuse to see Jilly later.

No one needed to tell him how ridiculous it was to carry a torch for Jillian Harper. He'd thought about no one but her the four years he was away, though he'd hoped it would help him let her go. But even being stationed as far away as Alaska hadn't done the trick. In fact, he bought a ring three months before he was scheduled to go home, determined to come back and make her fall in love with him.

Jilly had been there to welcome him back at his

homecoming party at the ranch. The town was planning a much bigger festivity for Paul's return from deployment a few months later, but he hadn't minded. He liked the smaller, more intimate event his cousin organized.

He came back a few weeks after Christmas, and still remembered the fuzzy blue sweater Jilly wore. How soft it felt against his neck when she wrapped her arms around him in a hug. He'd been foolish enough to think it meant something. Then she pulled back and something from her hand rubbed against his collarbone.

An engagement ring.

He hopped to his feet and prepared to take Buttercup home.

The fiancé lasted less than a couple of months before he left Jilly in Starlight to pursue some flashy corporate career in New York. He was glad to see him go, not because he was in love with her, but because the guy was all wrong for her. He didn't believe in her dreams, didn't support them.

If only the news of Paul hadn't come a few months later when she was finally able to move on from that heartbreak. Something always seemed to interfere when it came to them. He wondered if it would always be this way when it came to Jilly.

CHAPTER 3

*J*illian

"Okay, I sent the text," Jillian told Holly. "*Why* did I send Brantley a text?"

"Because he's going to be your plus one."

"*That's* the favor? I can't ask him to do that!" She paced in her studio, mortified at the very suggestion Holly had been brave enough to put to words. He would surely laugh at her all the way down the aisle.

"Why not?"

"We're friends, for one. He'd never go for it." They had a comfortable friendship. One she wasn't eager to muddy with a fake relationship request. "I can't ask him."

"Sure you can." Holly folded her arms and sat back in her chair, a devious smile falling across her lips. "He's the perfect candidate." She flashed fingers, counting on each one. "Single. Attractive. Cowboy. Your future stepmonster is going to crack her jaw on the tile floor when she first sets eyes on him."

"He's your *cousin*, Holly!"

"Oh, geez!" Holly wadded up a paper towel and tossed it at her, hitting her shoulder. "I don't mean *I* see him that way."

Milo barked, tail wagging at what he hoped was a new game. He pounced toward the balled-up paper, but she swiped it off the floor before he could get it.

She wouldn't admit out loud how very right her best friend was. Brantley turned more than a few heads. Jillian's too for a brief moment in time before he got the news about his brother. But she'd never admitted that to anyone. *We're friends!* Too good of friends to ever consider anything more.

Holly waved away her attempts at objecting. "There won't be a thing about him she can pick apart."

She felt a little sick to her stomach and couldn't even blame the pizza she'd barely touched. Brantley would never go for this. "What's in it for him?"

"Besides . . . never mind." Holly twirled a pencil in her hand, tapping it against her cheek a few times as she stared out the window. "I don't know. Maybe you should *ask* him?"

"What a time to be single," she muttered, clearing the plates. She put the pizza in the fridge in the studio's closet-turned-micro-kitchenette. "And might I add, *not* a super successful photographer."

"You just have to keep your dad and Stella away from here," Holly said. "They should be so busy it won't be a big deal. Why are you stressing so much over this?"

Jillian sank back into her chair. Milo rested his body against her legs, eyes searching for the wad of paper towels she had picked up off the floor. "It's Stella. She brings out the *worst* in me. I don't get why my dad wants to marry her. I never understood why they started dating." She had only been around Stella twice during this whirlwind romance. And both times, the woman found a way to make her feel insecure and insignificant about her achievements.

"It's what, a few days? It's your dad you're supporting," Holly reminded. "Then they'll go on some honeymoon and not bother you until at least Christmas."

She covered her face with her hands and moaned. "That's still too soon." The bells above the door jingled. Milo hopped up, on alert.

"Oh hey, Brantley," Holly greeted. "Jillian left you some pizza. Your favorite kind."

Brantley sported his crooked smile as he gave the

dog a solid neck and ear rub before finding his way to the fridge. "So you didn't let Milo down after all."

But her heart was beating much too fast for her typical type of retort. In fact, words in general didn't seem to form properly in her throat. This was a stupid idea. *Stupid, stupid idea.*

"What did you need?" Brantley crouched down and pulled out a plate from the mini fridge. Milo's tail went into overdrive, swishing against everything in its path as he followed Brantley to the table.

Holly locked eyes with her, a fierce look if she ever saw one in her sweet friend, and she rigidly nodded her head toward Brantley. "Ask him," came her whisper.

"Not now!" she whisper-shouted back.

Brantley set his plate on the table, but before taking a seat walked toward the backdrop to check the bracket he'd secured earlier. He tugged gently on the thick cloth, seemingly satisfied. "Something happen while I was gone?"

"No, not a thing," Jillian said. But her voice sounded awkward and squeaky, even to her.

Great. Now she'd have to face him. She was a terrible liar when it came to Brantley. She could tell her dad and Stella the most grandiose lies without blinking. But Brantley'd always been able to see through even her most basic fibs.

"Looks like the bracket's holding all right." He approached the table and fell into a chair next to her.

"Yep. It's been great."

"You're not going to warm that up?" Holly asked.

"Brantley likes his pizza cold," Jillian volunteered. "Don't ask, unless you have an hour for the debate that follows."

Brantley bit into his slice, swallowing before asking, "So this favor you needed?" He tossed a corner of pizza crust to Milo, who was now lying down beside his chair. "Another loose bracket or something?"

"I—" Her phone buzzed, the vibration always louder on this thin, hollow table. It was a text from Stella. With an attachment. She tried to leave it alone. She could look at it later. She'd endured enough bad news with learning they were moving the wedding. She wasn't ready to see how many days they were planning to spend in Starlight. If it was a single day over three, she might move to a new state.

"You gonna read that?" Holly asked. "It's probably about the wedding."

"Wedding?"

She took a deep breath, avoiding eye contact with her best friend. She might accidentally incinerate Holly with the laser beams that would surely shoot from her eyes. "My dad's."

"Oh, the one in Cancun next month?"

"That's the one." She unlocked her phone and waited for the attachment to download.

"Turns out it's in Starlight," Holly offered. "Next weekend."

Around another bite, Brantley asked, "Why the sudden change of plans?"

"Apparently *someone* tried to get out of Cancun," Holly answered before Jillian had a chance to defend herself.

Brantley turned in his chair, but not in time for her to bury her mortified expression in her hands. "You didn't."

Holly pushed back her chair, careful to avoid the eager dog behind her. Milo was hyper-focused on the pizza in Brantley's hand and uninterested in anyone who might be leaving. "I better be going. Got an afternoon date with a bunch of books and numbers. But Jillian can fill you in on all the drama her future stepmonster's been stirring up." Holly patted her shoulder as she passed. "And why she needs you to be her date. Toodles!"

"Your date?" Brantley echoed, pizza slice frozen in midair.

Her face had to be thirty-nine shades of red for how hot it felt. "She left out the detail about this being a big mess." She waved a hand toward the door as Holly disappeared, leaving her alone to deal with this debacle. If only she had RSVP'd yes to the original wedding, she could have saved herself all this trouble.

"Tell me more."

"Well, you know how Stella makes me a little crazy?"

"Heard a story or two." He tossed another bite of pizza crust to Milo. "Go on."

With a deep breath, she filled him in on the phone call.

"You really did RSVP no to your dad's wedding. Like, actually did that."

"Not my proudest moment, believe me." She fetched a couple of sodas from the fridge and slid one toward Brantley. "Anyway, the last time I visited them I may have embellished how great things are for me."

"So naturally, you need *me* to be your fake date." Brantley cracked open his can and took a swig. Confusion and a sprinkle of curiosity danced in his dark eyes.

"Could I bribe you with a week of free breakfasts?" she offered. But when he didn't seem amused, she kept on. "My dad doesn't know Jason and I ever broke up."

Brantley's eyes grew a little wide. "I'm not pretending to be that jerk." His firm tone didn't leave room for negotiation. "Don't you have any other old boyfriends who owe you a favor? Maybe a new one?"

Ignoring the jabs in his comment, she said again, "He doesn't know we broke up. But he can't even remember his name. You wouldn't have to pretend to be anybody other than yourself. The only fabrication is that we've been together for two years."

Brantley choked on a sip of his soda and reached for a napkin. Once he caught his breath, he asked, "You need me to pretend I've been dating you. For *two* years?" He shook his head. "I can't do that, Jilly. I just . . . I wasn't even living in Starlight two years ago, remember?"

"They don't know that."

"If you need a fake two-year boyfriend, there're plenty of men in Starlight willing to play the part. Ask one of them."

"I'm not asking anyone else." The tiny bubble of hope that he might somehow find this amusing and agree for the sake of a few good laughs died. She slid out of her seat at the table and fell into her chair at her desk. She could at least pretend to edit photos. "I can't show up to that wedding without a date. Stella will want to push her arrogant *photographer* nephew on me again." She closed her eyes and sucked in a deep breath. "It's a long, mortifying story. Forget it, though. I'm sorry I even asked."

"Wouldn't it be better to tell the truth?"

She shrugged, stupid tears pricking at the corners of her eyes. Not from disappointment. Oh no, these puppies were from humiliation. "They also think I have a super successful photography business in an elite studio. That I'm booked up for months."

"Oh, Jilly." Somehow Brantley had moved across the room without making a sound.

Too shaken to risk messing up her real estate photos, she took to scrolling through her phone instead. But one glance at the itinerary Stella sent her made Jillian's heart drop to her toes. "They're coming tomorrow."

"But the wedding isn't until next weekend."

She sprang from her chair to pace. Milo, poor confused dog, kept bouncing his gaze between her and the table where the last piece of pizza waited. "That's an entire week. I can't handle Stella for a whole week. How am I going to keep them away from here for that long? I just . . . Brantley, break my leg."

"What?"

"I need a way to get out of this."

"I'm not breaking anybody's leg!"

"You're right. Bad idea." The pacing, as well as her erratic breathing, quickened. "Plus, that wouldn't stop Stella from smothering me with passive-aggressive insults." How she longed to be out at the lake right now with the fresh air to calm her frayed nerves. "I'll Google the most contagious diseases." She darted for her computer, but Brantley caught her shoulders and held on tightly as she squirmed.

"Jilly."

"Okay, just illnesses. They'll never believe I contracted a disease overnight."

"Jillian." Brantley shook her shoulders. Lightly, but it was enough to stop her. She met his eyes. Always such kind eyes. Compassionate. "I need a few minutes to think this through."

"Okay."

He moved past her toward the door, stepping outside onto the covered porch and closing the door behind him.

"Should I pack our bags now?" she asked Milo, as she sank back into the chair. The dog let out a whine, hoping for more pizza. "Maybe we should try Arizona. Or head east to Maine."

Jillian tried to return to editing the listing photos she started before the pizza arrived, but it was no use. Instead, she took to cleaning up the lunch mess. And once that was done, she started in sweeping, despite having swept the floor first thing that morning.

"I'll do it." Brantley startled her with his sudden, ninja-like appearance. *Had the bells even jingled?*

Her words escaped as hardly a whisper, "You will?" But her relief was thunderous. She considered throwing her arms around his neck and hugging the air clean out of him.

"But there're conditions." Hugging the broom handle to her chest instead, she waited with attentive eyes to hear what this was going to cost. "First, I need your help exercising a horse this week."

Though she spent a lot of time around horses—cleaning out their stalls, feeding and watering them, brushing them—it had been years she'd ridden one. A pretty bad fall had scared her enough to keep her on the ground around them. But Brantley didn't know anything about that. He'd been away in the Army when that happened. "Okay," she agreed, hoping she'd managed to keep any quiver out of her voice. "Sure. I can do that."

"Good. But that's not all." Of course it wasn't. "I need your help with a picture."

"You want me to take one?" she asked.

"No, I want you to teach me how to take it. It's, uh, for my mom. Surprise."

That didn't seem too terrible. She could help him take a few pictures one day, edit his favorite. "Of what?"

"The sunrise."

She wasn't crazy about the idea. She was already short enough on sleep as it was. But it wasn't the worst thing he could ask her to help him with. "Okay."

"There's one thing, though."

"What?"

"It's a little bit of a ride."

"Okay."

"And a hike. Might be easiest to camp out there the night before."

She shook her head. "I don't do camping." Though she'd lived in Starlight several years now, she hadn't grown up here. They'd lived in cities until she turned fifteen. "I don't do bugs and creepy crawlies and sleeping on the ground. Nope."

"Then find yourself a new fake boyfriend."

"There isn't another spot?"

"It has to be this one."

She could tell—something in his steely eyes—that this spot was important to him. She wanted to ask, but pushing right now might leave her in a complete bind. "Fine." She couldn't believe she was about to agree to this. "Fine, I'll do it."

"Are you sure? There might still be time to arrange that broken leg."

"Ha ha." She really was in no position to argue. She needed him to agree now or she'd be dateless for Stella's dinner tomorrow—the first of many items on that irritating itinerary. "Any more demands?"

Brantley folded his arms and leaned back against the wall, a mischievous twinkle in his eyes. "As a matter of fact, there *is* one more."

She had come too far in this negotiation to shut it down now. "What?"

"I'll take that week of free breakfast you offered."

"But—"

"I'll be by every morning at seven." With what appeared to be a victorious smile, he extended his hand and asked, "Do we have a deal?"

She knew this favor would cost her, but she hadn't expected him to enjoy it so much. She shook his hand. "Deal."

CHAPTER 4

Brantley

This wasn't the first terrible idea Brantley had ever entertained.

No.

There'd been that decision to have a few too many drinks the night before a five-mile battalion run his first year in the Army.

He once thought eating nothing but peanut butter and jelly sandwiches would be a great way to save money when he was penny-pinching, saving up for a motorcycle that ended up dying ten miles from town on its first ride.

But perhaps the worst of them all was agreeing to

be Jillian Harper's fake serious boyfriend of two years.

Those tears she tried to hide, though. He couldn't have ignored those no matter how cold-hearted he pretended to be. He'd overheard more than one phone conversation in which her future stepmother repeatedly put down Jillian's life choices.

"You sure about this?" Hudson Ross sat next to him at the bar of the Starlight Grill.

The two had become acquainted a couple of years ago when they were both conned into helping with the city park renovation project. But then, no one said no to Violet Livingston when she had an idea that would benefit the community. Especially when she so willingly bribed every last helper with her famous pies.

Having arrived first, Brantley had ordered them each a beer. He took a long pull from his cold one. "Nope."

"How did—"

"Don't know, man."

"She doesn't know—"

"No."

Hudson didn't need to utter the truth out loud for them both to know what it was. Jillian had no idea what Brantley felt for her. Very few people did. Hudson was among those rare folks he'd confided in. Spending time with Jillian—that was the easy part. He could play the part of the doting boyfriend.

Jillian would be the actress, believing they were both playing a part. *Terrible idea.* Would he survive the sting once the wedding festivities were over and she expected everything to go back to normal?

"Maybe you've found yourself an opportunity."

Hudson raised his beer in what Brantley thought might be a toast. But he left his glass untouched on the counter and tapped at the bar stool with his boot instead. "Opportunity?"

"Sure." Hudson folded his arms against the counter and leaned on them. "Show her how things *could* be. Make her fall for you, man."

"Nah." Could he really pull that off? "You think?"

"Why not?" Hudson took another pull of his beer. "What do you have to lose? If Jillian doesn't go for it, things go back to where they are now. Easy enough to keep your distance on a ranch that size."

He couldn't argue that logic. The Maxwell Ranch was one of the biggest in the county. If he wanted to avoid Jillian, it wouldn't take much effort. In fact, it took a whole lot more to run into her so often.

He was sure he wouldn't sleep tonight. Too much to mull over. Jillian's dad and fiancée arrived in Starlight tomorrow afternoon. They were expecting Jillian and her *boyfriend* to join them for dinner. The noise of the restaurant crowd hummed around him, adding to the spinning sensation in his mind. He couldn't quite decide how he felt.

"What's on that mind of yours, West?" Hudson asked after a long silence.

"Is it weird to be nervous about meeting her dad?"

Hudson gave a hearty laugh at that. "I'd be nervous to meet him. Heard he's about the size of a brick house and pretty protective of his baby girl. Carries a shotgun in the back window of his truck. The man eats bullets for breakfast."

"Are you—" But he caught himself before he said something even more embarrassing. Of course those things weren't true. Jillian had shown him a picture of her dad a couple of weeks ago. He was on the tall side, but nothing quite like a brick house.

Jillian never said much about her dad, but everyone knew he left town before she graduated high school. He wondered what motivated her to lie about how her life was going. She was twenty-four, two years younger than he was. They both had so much time to figure out life.

"Relax, man," Hudson said. "From the sound of things, he'll have his hands full enough with that fiancée."

He decided the best tactic for saving a shred of his dignity was to change subjects. "How're things at the ranch?" Hudson worked on the Livingston Ranch, one of the other large ranches in the area.

"Busy as always. You should come out tomorrow if you have some time. We've been working on the first cut. Might put together a bonfire after. Violet always makes a huge spread to feed the helpers."

"Hay baling already? Feels like the summer's running away."

"Bring Jillian too if you want." Hudson emptied his beer and stretched as he stood. "Ronnie wants me to come over for dinner tonight, so I need to head out. Perks of having your little sister living in town—you never go hungry." He clapped Brantley hard on the shoulder. "Think on what I said. Could be your best shot."

He took his time finishing his beer, the muffled blend of conversations happening around him to keep him company. He had no urgency to get home. He didn't even have a goldfish waiting for him. *Maybe I should get a dog.*

"Need another?" the bartender asked when he slid his empty bottle away.

He considered saying yes, until a slender blonde fell into the empty stool next to him. Her thick perfume suffocated him in a cloud as she turned a flirty smile his way. "Brantley West. What brings Starlight's most eligible bachelor out alone on a beautiful night like this?"

She was a Starlight transplant, new to town as of a couple of years ago. Any number of men might have been flattered—flustered even—to receive such avid attention from Corrine Daily. But he was tired. She'd been trying to wear him down for months.

"Just finishing up a beer." He slipped a ten-dollar bill toward the bartender to cover the beer he bought for Hudson as well. "Have a good evening, Corrine." He'd started by calling her Ms. Daily when she began her pursuit, but that only seemed to entice her more.

"Leaving already?" She snaked both hands around one of his biceps. He had to give her credit for her tough but failed effort to yank him back in the stool he just abandoned. "Won't you join me for one little drink?"

"Can't."

But Corrine wasn't willing to let go, and she shoved her cleavage clear up against his arm. Her perfume was too much; he might sneeze. "You wouldn't make a lady drink alone?"

He briefly wondered what an episode like this might look like to Jillian's dad when they were supposed to have been dating for two years. He found himself glancing around the room, searching for a man who matched a fuzzy memory from a photo he'd only glimpsed. He wasn't as convinced as Hudson that this was *the* opportunity, but if there was even a sliver of hope that Jillian could fall for him, he didn't need Corrine stirring complications into the mix.

"Sorry, I have to get back to the ranch." Wriggling free of her vise-like grip, he dug another five out of his wallet and slapped it on the counter. "Your first one's on me, though."

"You can't keep running from me forever, Brantley West," she cooed.

He didn't have a rebuttal to that, so he lifted his hat from the hook beneath the bar and put it on, leaving Corrine with a half-hearted wave. He couldn't get outside fast enough, into the fresh air that cleansed his senses of that thick perfume. It clung to the sleeve of his shirt anyway.

He swung by the gas station to pick up a bag of his favorite chips. He didn't recognize the cashier tonight, and for that he was grateful. He was exhausted from all the talking, and wanted only to lounge on the couch and binge watch crime shows on Netflix.

Twenty minutes into an episode of *Cold Blooded*, and less than two minutes from discovering whodunnit, someone pounded at his front door. From the frantic nature, Brantley feared bad news. Had something happened to Edie?

"Hey, is—"

"Brantley! You're home." Jillian pushed her way past him, inviting herself in out of the cool evening air. Milo shoved his way in right behind. Her cheeks held a bit of pink to them, as if she'd gone for a long walk.

"Is everything okay?"

"How could it be?" She paced in short strides beside him "My dad and his fiancée will be in town in less than twenty-four hours and we don't even have our cover stories!" She kept at it until he reached out and bookended her shoulders. His fingers tingled as they always did on the rare occasions they touched.

"Hey." He waited for her to stop bouncing her eyes around his living room and look at him. It occurred to him she might never have seen the inside of his cabin. He rarely had visitors, and he made sure most women didn't know where he lived. "We can sort this out."

"Yeah?"

"Why don't you sit down and I'll grab you something to drink."

"Do you have a bottle of whiskey?" He opened his mouth to respond but found he didn't know how. She held up her hands. "Kidding. I'll take whatever you got. If it has alcohol in it, that's better yet."

"Did you drive?"

She shook her head, the messy bun loosening and dropping from its spot atop her head. "Walked." He longed to slip off her hair tie. It'd been so long since she let down her auburn hair. Instead, he shoved his hands into his front pockets and headed toward the kitchen. Milo followed him like a shadow.

"Sorry, buddy. Don't really have much to share. And one of you needs to be sober enough to walk home."

"You watch these?" she called from his couch.

"All the time."

"And you don't have nightmares?"

He dug around in the fridge and found a can of Coke and one beer. He pulled two glasses from his cupboard and carried the haul to his coffee table. "Not usually."

"I should probably write this down, huh? If we'd been dating two years, I'd know you like to watch crime shows." Milo trotted around the coffee table and rested his head against Jillian's knees.

He held up both drink options in offering, and she pointed to the beer. "Well, you know now." He poured half the bottle in a mug and slid it across the table. "We can share. It's my last one." If those panic-stricken eyes were any indication, her stress level probably couldn't tolerate a full beer anyway.

"Thanks." She curled her feet under her legs, leaning against the arm of his plush gray couch. "I'm sorry. I should've called or something. I just . . . I took Milo for a walk and ended up here."

For how long had he dreamed that very scenario? But of course, in his fantasy she didn't end up on his doorstep wanting to discuss details of a fake relationship. He took a swig of his beer. "You've got about an hour before I won't be able to keep my eyes open," he lied. "So let's figure out this story of ours."

"You make it sound so simple."

"Doesn't have to be complicated."

"Guess not." He longed to take her in his arms to soothe her, but here behind closed doors where there was no one to pretend for, he wasn't sure how she would react to such a gesture.

"Jilly, everything's going to be okay. It's only a week. Next time they visit, you can tell them you dumped me and it broke my heart so badly I left town or something."

A weak smile finally broke across her lips, and he had to look away before she caught him staring.

If only his own words didn't echo the possibility he feared the most.

CHAPTER 5

Milo sat beside the car patiently as Jillian hopped up onto the door frame. She unstrapped her paddleboard from the roof of her SUV. The long powder blue board barely fit, and only by removing the car's radio antenna. Small price to pay for freedom.

There were two things that could calm even her most frayed nerves and bring a sense of calm.

The first was photography. Finding that perfect frame. Capturing that flawless, unfiltered moment of emotion. She first discovered this joy when she was fifteen, right after her dad left. When she lost herself in the pursuit of capturing perfect pictures, it helped her forget he left her behind.

Though these last few years, she'd mostly been taking photos of real estate properties and professional headshots. She needed a larger portfolio to convince clients to trust her with important days like weddings, graduations, and anniversaries. But with limited opportunities to grow her portfolio, it was an uphill battle.

Her second stress reliever was paddle boarding.

"Looks like we have the lake to ourselves today, huh, buddy?"

Brantley practically insisted she spend the morning on the lake before she left his cabin last night. "Go do something that relaxes you first thing," he'd ordered her. "I'll pick you up for dinner at six-thirty." Coming from him, those words felt strange. Foreign, even. How many women in town would kill to hear those very words from Brantley West? Would this fake relationship affect his dating possibilities? Worse yet, she hoped she didn't become some sort of target.

With any luck, most of the town would never know about any of this. But Starlight was a small community, and once word got out, it would circle like a hawk.

Jillian shuddered. "No more thoughts about that until we leave," she said to Milo. "Deal?"

The dog hopped up to all fours, tail wagging in

earnest, though it was because the board was down, and he knew what that meant.

It had taken an entire summer to train Milo on her paddleboard. He wasn't too keen on swimming or being submerged in water. But he loved perching on the board and observing the world around him. It was his insatiable curiosity of the things lurking *in* the water that had capsized them dozens of times and nearly made her give up. But by the end of that first summer, he had it figured out.

Now he was content to climb onto the board and plop down on its nose before it pushed off into the water. Sometimes he even fell asleep as she slowly guided them around the peaceful lake.

In the summer, this lake could be a crowded place. But luckily only a few were out on the water today—one kayaker and a couple in a canoe off in the distance. Sometimes she found someone out fishing, but the locals knew this was the worst lake to catch anything worth keeping.

She slipped off her sandals and left them on the sandy shore. Once Milo was situated, she pushed off far enough into the water to pry the board free with her paddle, but not so far that she'd soak her shorts.

Out on the lake, stress melted away. There was no wedding, no future stepmonster, no returning dad who'd abandoned her in this same town coming to see her fabricated version of success. Certainly no fake relationship.

Like Milo, she was at peace.

In the center of the lake, she pulled the paddle from the water and set it across her lap. She allowed her eyes to drift closed, to soak in the warmth the sun had to offer.

As she did each time, she envisioned a future in which she ran a successful photography business. A calendar booked weeks, even months, out. Clients tearing up with happiness at the amazing photos that captured the heart of who they were. It was a dream she kept close to her heart.

But today, no matter what images she conjured, Brantley slipped into each one. What had she let Holly talk her into? Brantley was . . . well, he was quite attractive. She had never failed to notice that detail—like any woman in Starlight. But they'd developed such a solid friendship since he moved back. Nothing would convince her that was worth jeopardizing.

Once she'd thought differently. But fate had stepped in and intervened, giving her a warning sign to step back before she did something reckless.

"Ugh, this is such a bad idea!"

Milo looked up from the board with a tilted head, wondering why their peaceful afternoon had been disrupted. He cautiously stood and maneuvered until he lay with his head in her lap.

"Hey, buddy." She rubbed his neck until his eyes squeezed shut.

They floated until the sun no longer had clouds to hide behind. Until she could no longer put off getting ready for tonight's dinner.

———

Jillian wiped sweaty palms against her jeans. She debated—repeatedly—whether to wear her dark-washed skinny jeans or a dress to this dinner. Holly pointed out she'd be the most comfortable in jeans. "Stella will probably have a comment on your wardrobe anyway. Might as well wear what makes you happy."

"You okay?" Brantley asked before they stepped inside the Starlight Grill.

"Yeah."

"Remember, you have that class to teach tonight. We can only stay an hour."

There was something oddly relieving in the way he said *we*. As if they were a team, in this together. "This is your last chance to run," she teased, but her words wobbled with nerves.

"I haven't run away from you yet, Jilly." He took her hand between both of his, patting it. "Probably should pretend to be a couple, right?"

"You're about to break a lot of hearts in Starlight." She had never thought about that reper-cussion. Of course not. She'd only been looking out for herself. Brantley didn't go on many dates—or any she could recall in the last several months. But he was good at keeping secrets. Maybe he took his dates out of town. "Are you okay with—"

"It'll be a relief, believe me." His words sounded filled with truth, and a bit winded. "We can deal with the aftermath later. After the wedding."

She squeezed his hand in thanks, aware how warm his skin was against hers. Odd. She'd never noticed that before. She'd always been careful to avoid touching him, worried it would weaken her resolve to keep him at arm's length. She forced herself to disconnect from any lingering thoughts about holding hands with him, and what it might mean.

Inside the restaurant, she squared her shoulders, tucked a stray hair from her bun—a little bit less messy than usual—behind her ear, and marched forward.

"Sweet Pea!" Rodney Harper, tall and thin, wrapped his long arms around her and squeezed her against him as though she were still the fifteen-year-old he left behind. She had visited her dad a few times since that day he left, but this was the first time he was back *here*.

"Dad." When he still hadn't let go, she patted his shoulder. "Dad. I can't breathe."

"Oh, sorry." He released her, and his eyes immediately traveled to Brantley. His head bobbed in exaggerated obviousness as he looked him up and down a few times. "You must be the *boyfriend.*"

She should've warned Brantley how her dad would be a little overprotective. "Dad, this is Brantley."

"Mr. Harper, it's a pleasure to meet you." Brantley extended his hand and didn't even blink while he waited an uncomfortable amount of time for her dad to finally shake it. "Jillian's told me so much about you."

"Where's Stella?" she asked, hoping to save Brantley from a line of interrogatory questioning for as long as possible.

"In the powder room. She'll be right with us. Please, sit."

Even if it were only a few minutes of reprieve, she would gladly take them. Stella never strayed far from her dad, and likely wouldn't leave his side the rest of the time they were in town.

"You sure got in quick." She slid into the booth first, followed by Brantley. She was acutely aware how close he sat. Any other time she would've sat away from him, but this fake relationship had to appear convincing. If it didn't, Stella would call it out in a heartbeat. "They let you take off work whenever you want these days?"

"Oh, he doesn't work anymore." Stella's shrill voice boomed behind them. "I talked him into retiring a month ago."

"What?" She narrowed her eyes at her dad as she unrolled her napkin and spread it in her lap. He may have bounced around from different jobs and passions when she was growing up, but she was certain he'd found his calling with commercial real estate. "I thought you loved your work."

Stella stood near her seat, her eyes laser-focused on Brantley. "You must be the mysterious boyfriend we've heard *so* much about." She eyed him like an item from the dessert menu.

Her dad slid over, allowing Stella to scoot in and Jillian averted her eyes. After viewing the perky chest resting on the table like a tacky shelf arrangement, she wasn't sure she'd be able to eat.

"Why did you retire?" she asked, as her last question was ignored.

"It was time." Stella turned her chest toward her fiancé, pushing a rolled napkin on the way, and petted his arm. "He worked so much. But now we have time to do all the things we've been putting off."

Jillian's fists balled the napkin in her lap. No doubt Stella had talked him into spending his hard-earned retirement on frivolous outings and vacations. "Dad, are you happy not working?" She didn't know why she bothered asking. Even if he wasn't happy, he'd never be honest; that was, if Stella allowed him to answer for himself.

"Oh, trust me, Jill, he's happy."

"Jillian," she corrected through gritted teeth and

a forced smile that made her face stretch painfully. The waitress saved her, delivering a tray of iced water.

"Do you have sparkling water?" Stella asked.

The waitress blinked, glanced at Rodney, then finally said, "I'm sorry, no. I can get you something else to drink?"

"How about a cosmo? Do you have cosmos?"

"I'll check with the bartender." She nodded toward Rodney, but before he could place his own order, Stella ordered him an iced tea.

She stared across the table in disbelief. He never drank iced tea, even if it was offered. Years of various neighborhood block parties and people offering him iced tea flashed through her mind, but the memory of Dad turning it down was always the same.

Brantley patted her thigh. "Jilly, what do you want to drink?" Heat rushed up her neck at the realization she'd missed the waitress's attempt to gain her attention. It had to be that, and not the heated hand sliding from her leg. Her nerves were simply unsettled with her dad and Stella in town. That and nothing more.

"Light beer. Whatever's on tap."

Stella scoffed as if the drink was the vilest thing she could have ordered, and it made her smile so big her toes curled. "You really drink that stuff?"

"Sure do." *Own it.* That's what Holly had repeated to her on the phone as she dressed for dinner. No matter how much Stella tried to put down anything she liked or accomplished, she needed to own it.

"Jilly here is full of surprises." Brantley flashed her a smirk. "It's one of my favorite things about her." His words sounded sincere, but she had to wonder *how* he meant them.

After the drinks arrived and orders were in, Dad fired away a string of questions at Brantley. She found she knew a lot less about him than she realized. But she kept her lips sealed in a smile as if she'd always known he was a helicopter door gunner during his time in Iraq or that his family once traveled across the country in an RV when he was ten.

Brantley continued, right on through their appetizer being delivered. She was so engrossed in his stories of a family he rarely mentioned, she didn't realize how quickly she was consuming her beer until Brantley leaned his head in and whispered against her ear.

"Jilly, you need to slow down. Your students can't have a lightweight teaching class."

His breath tickled her ear and for a solitary moment, she forgot anyone else was around. When was the last time someone had this kind of intoxicating effect on her? Surely it was the alcohol. At least the empty glass in front of her seemed to imply as much. "Okay." She forced her hands into her lap.

The server delivered their plates, and she

wondered how she missed her dad ordering nothing but a hearty salad. It didn't even have steak on it, only pieces of grilled chicken. She wanted to say something. This wasn't Dad. Who had Stella been changing him into?

"How's business?" he asked, poking at the greens he didn't seem too crazy about eating. "I hear you're pretty in demand these days."

"Well, a small town like this probably doesn't have a lot of other options, do they?" Stella sipped her cosmo, wearing that sweet, sickening smile that always played at innocence no matter how lethal her insinuations. A smile that reminded Jillian she and Brantley were acting for the sake of her dad. Without Brantley beside her, she wasn't sure she could tolerate Stella, even in small doses.

"It's quite a competitive market, believe it or not." Brantley took his time cutting into his steak, demonstrating a kind of patience she could only hope to master. "Jillian does quite a lot, even teaches. In fact, she has a class tonight."

"You do?"

"Yes, we have half an hour before I need to be there." She smiled, knowing Brantley was only trying to help. But the less they talked about her business, the less likely the topic of visiting the studio would come up. The last she told them, a newer, bigger studio was undergoing renovations.

"So," Stella said, "what kind of class?"

The best thing she could do was change the subject to anything else. Stella would surely have some demeaning comment about her beginner's smartphone photography class taught mostly to senior citizens. "Did you know Brantley built his cabin himself?"

"Did you, now?" Rodney asked, seemingly more interested in that detail than the photography class.

"Yes, sir."

There. She did know *something*. "It's gorgeous." Though her first visit was only last night, and she was much too distracted to take in many details, she recalled polished hardwood floors and black granite countertops. Maybe even a dark gray accent wall.

"That's amazing," Stella cooed, her cleavage bouncing with her interest. "Maybe we'll have to stop by and see it before the week is over." She clapped her hands together at a revelation. "You could have us over for dinner!"

Well, this was a disaster. "Brantley's very busy. I don't think—"

"Oh, come on. One little dinner. We're easy to please." Stella sent an exaggerated wink across the table. Reached for her cosmo. And emptied the glass.

Even her dad looked a little embarrassed at the self-invitation. "Darling, I think we'll be plenty busy this week." He patted her hand, but she pulled it away. "Brantley sounds pretty busy himself."

"I'll see what we can do," Brantley offered.

"I'm holding you to it. Maybe Tuesday night or something? We don't have to pick up my nephew from the airport until Wednesday. Jill, you remember my dear nephew, Chad? He's so excited to see you again! Such a talented photographer."

Jillian remembered, all right. During a visit to see Dad, Stella invited Chad over, too. Tried on multiple occasions to stick the two of them together. Alone. Chad was nice, but he was arrogant. Blunt. Uncomfortable to be around. Thought he knew everything there was to know about photography, and wouldn't accept anything she had to say on the subject. It'd been the main reason she'd talked nonstop about a boyfriend she no longer had.

"Chad?" Brantley's voice was low against her ear.

"Don't ask."

"Sounds like we'll play it by ear," Rodney said, taking the check the server brought for the table and leaving his credit card inside. "I'm sure we can figure something out."

A trickle of panic crept in. Brantley's cabin was on the other side of the Maxwell Ranch, but if her dad and Stella got lost, they might drive right by her cabin with its gigantic sign, *Jillian's Photography*. She reached for her glass, wishing it would magically refill. This entire lie might unravel despite her best efforts.

"We'll need directions," Stella said.

Brantley made an exaggerated gesture of looking at his watch. "I have to get Jilly off to her class. Can't let the teacher be late now, can I?"

She let the tension in her shoulders drop a notch, relieved for the exit. "Yes, I do have to get going. Dad, I'm sorry to rush out—"

"We knew you were a busy woman before we moved the wedding, Sweet Pea."

"Maybe we can get together?" Stella looked at her directly. "How about pedicures tomorrow? Surely you can squeeze in some time for pampering."

Her Monday, outside of preparing breakfast for Brantley and fitting in one real estate listing shoot, was wide open. She hadn't even been able to get a stray shift at the diner. "I . . ." How was she going to get out of this one? Pedicures, just her and Stella? Surely she'd insert her foot so far in her mouth they'd kick her out of the wedding. She couldn't be trusted alone with her future stepmonster.

"Honey, we have to help the Livingstons tomorrow, remember? They're baling hay."

"Baling hay?" Stella repeated the words as if he'd said *alien invasion* instead. "You don't *really* do any of that, do you? Him"—she waved a hand at Brantley as if the checkered button-down shirt and Wranglers said it all—"I believe *he* knows how to work with hands. But you, Jill?"

"It's Jillian, dear," her dad corrected.

"I assure you, *Jillian's* not afraid to get her hands

dirty." Brantley slid out of the booth, dragging her with him by the arm. "But she'll be manning her camera."

"A photoshoot?" Rodney asked.

"Yep."

"I need to get Jilly to her class. We'll see you both soon. Stella, Mr. Harper, it was a pleasure." He shook Rodney's hand and Jillian got in a quick hug before Brantley ushered them both out of the Starlight Grill. It wasn't until they were driving away in the truck that she was finally able to breathe.

CHAPTER 6

$\mathcal{B}$rantley

Some things Brantley would never understand.

He paced his kitchen the next morning, waiting on the coffee to brew. The sun hadn't yet come up, but one by one the stars disappeared as the sky lightened. He had a pretty decent sunrise view off his back deck when he took time to enjoy it. That's why he built it that way.

Sunrises had always been Paul's thing.

That Paul was no longer here to enjoy them . . . that was something he hadn't quite come to terms with. The *why* of it all.

The aroma of his favorite dark roast filled his open-concept cabin. Only an island separated the kitchen from the living and dining areas. He designed it this way after spending a year living in a Conex overseas, confined to a twenty-by-seven-foot dwelling he shared with another soldier. He never again wanted to feel that claustrophobic.

The quiet usually brought him comfort, but this morning it was lonely. He found himself eagerly awaiting the ticking of the clock; when the hands found seven and he could join Jillian for breakfast. He didn't care if she only managed to scrounge up a bowl of cereal or instant oatmeal for him. Breakfast wasn't what really mattered.

His mind kept wandering back to dinner the night before. It had done that all night long as he drifted in and out of sleep.

He had been striving to get an accurate read on Rodney Harper throughout the entire meal. He seemed to genuinely love his daughter and want the best for her. He couldn't imagine the man being disappointed in Jillian's current achievements, even if he were to discover that she was still working her way toward the success she already claimed to have. Stella, however . . . Now, she could present a problem.

Coffee done, he poured what would fit into a Thermos, stirred in hazelnut creamer, and emptied the rest of his carafe into a mug. Rodney had certainly been protective of Jillian when they met. He wondered what it would take to win his approval.

But then he reminded himself that in a little over a week, it might not matter.

"I need to get a dog," he muttered.

His last months in the Army, he had yearned terribly for the slower pace of his former life in Wyoming. The quiet. The serenity. The rewarding, if not weary, feeling of a hard day's work done on the ranch. He'd missed home.

Enlisting had been a whimsical decision, made after one of Paul's visits home for Christmas. He talked about the military with such excitement and pride, and everyone around him became instantly enamored by his every word. When Brantley talked of his life on the ranch to his brother, that glow of excitement faded from Paul's eyes.

Half a cup of coffee left and a good thirty minutes before he could bother Jillian, he followed his hallway behind the kitchen to the smallest of the three bedrooms. He rarely opened this door. Would've locked it if he'd installed the right type of doorknob.

Talking about the military last night at dinner brought back a lot, even if he kept most of it to himself. He'd joined the Army hoping to finally win his brother's approval. Hoping to make his family as proud of him as they were of Paul. But their reaction hadn't been as supportive as he expected. Quite the opposite, really.

Dozens of large landscape photographs filled the

room. Some of the framed shots he'd hung on the walls. Most leaned in stacks against the walls or waited piled on the desk. Every picture was of the sunrise in a different location throughout the world.

Paul's photographs.

His throat constricted; his feet shackled in place in the doorway. It was all he had left of his brother, and only because Paul left his collection in his care prior to his deployment.

"I don't trust them in a storage unit," Paul said when Brantley was packing up a trailer, preparing to drive four days from Alaska to Wyoming. "I'll come get them when I get back, after we take our trip."

Then Paul was killed in action, only one month before he was due to return home.

The tightening in his chest was warning enough for him to close the door.

The picture he wanted Jillian to help him take wasn't for his mom, though after his conversation with Edie and the promise he made to call, he might make a second copy for her. This photo was a peace offering of sorts. Paul had never considered photography more than a hobby, but anyone who saw his photographs couldn't deny his talent.

He emptied the remaining coffee down the sink. It'd gone cold.

Leaving now would make him early for breakfast at Jillian's, but he couldn't stay here. He'd do the chores on his list after he left her studio, before they headed over to the Livingston Ranch. Holly already had a crew appointed to move the big herd into the north pasture today. He only needed to see to the horses and the stable. Lightest list of tasks she'd given him in over a year.

The Maxwell Ranch spanned more than twelve thousand acres. Much of that land was pasture, mountains, and streams. The main house, where Holly resided and a handful of cabins was located, to include the one Jillian rented, were situated on the west end of the ranch. He had purposely built his cabin on the ranch's east side, where only a couple of other cabins were scattered. Despite the distance, it never took him more than seven or eight minutes to cruise from his cabin to Jillian's.

He hadn't even rolled to stop before he spotted Milo's mug in the window, golden tail swishing playfully. The soft glow of light seemed to imply Jillian was awake and hadn't forgotten their breakfast arrangement.

In truth, he rarely ate breakfast, though after she made the offer, the temptation to see her every morning was too much to pass up. Should anyone ask, he'd deny that with his last breath. With any luck, once the wedding was over, she would realize she missed him coming around.

He knocked twice, then let himself into the studio. Her living quarters were on the upper level, a snug loft with a dinky kitchenette and a bathroom so small one could hardly move around in it. He only knew because he'd renovated the cabin for her. The upstairs apartment had only been intended for occasional use, but once her fiancé left, she'd moved in full time.

"Hey." Jillian flashed a smile, but the weariness in her eyes overshadowed it. "Got your breakfast upstairs, staying warm." Milo leaned up against his legs, demanding a dose of attention and a solid neck rub.

"You sleep any?"

Jillian shrugged and moved toward the stairs. "Some." She vanished up the stairs, Milo on her heels at the prospect of a handout.

Unable to sit still, he checked the backdrop again. The bracket held, as he knew it would. He scanned the room, looking for other things that might need repair. When he fixed up the cabin for her, he'd torn the interior down to its studs.

"I hope you're okay with scrambled eggs and toast." Jillian slid two plates onto the table. "I haven't had a chance to get groceries." Milo followed her to her desk. She pulled open the bottom drawer and riffled through its contents.

"You'll need your camera today," Brantley said.

"To bale hay?"

"To take pictures."

"I don't know, Brantley." She dropped two sets of

plastic silverware onto the table. "It was a good excuse, but I'll only be in the way."

"If you don't want to take photos, then come lend a hand. There's plenty that needs done," he suggested, though he couldn't picture her driving a tractor or tossing bales onto a trailer. Maybe it would be better if she hid out at the cabin or snuck away to the lake again.

She filled two mugs with coffee and joined him at the table. "What would they even do with a bunch of pictures of that? It's not exactly a celebration or memorable event. Just something that has to get done a couple times a year."

"It was an idea to get you out of bonding time with Stella." Brantley pushed his scrambled eggs around on his plate before scooping a bunch onto his fork. He'd be lying to himself if he admitted he wasn't disappointed. Why couldn't she see this for the opportunity it was?

"When do you need help exercising that horse?" she asked, obviously ravenous. But she barely touched her food last night at the restaurant, so he wasn't surprised.

"Wednesday, I think," he said. "But I'll have to see what Holly has on the schedule." He wanted to give her ample time to get used to the idea before rushing her into it. He could take her riding at any point, but she needed time to confront her fears. Fears she didn't even know he knew about.

"My week is unfortunately light." She pushed a stray long bang from her face, one he'd been eyeing since she brought the plates over. "Just let me know when you need me."

"Jilly." When she refused to look up, he reached a hand across the table and covered hers. He fought to control his breathing at her touch. "Jilly, you're a very talented photographer." She had never really known Paul. Likely didn't know about his hobby, or that he taught Brantley a few things about a great photo. And her skills could rival Paul's any day. "Great things are going to happen for you if you keep at it, I know."

"Thanks for saying so." She pulled her hand back, quick at collecting their empty plates.

"I really think you should come with me to the Livingston Ranch. You never know what might inspire you there."

At the foot of the stairs, she stopped. Turning a look over her shoulder, she met his gaze and ventured, "You think they'll mind?"

A victorious smile fell across his lips, but he hid it with a sip of coffee. "I'll be back in a couple hours to pick you up."

CHAPTER 7

Jillian

Jillian tugged on a worn cowgirl boot. A pair she hadn't worn since her high school days, when her mom thought it would be good for her to work summers outside, on a ranch. Though, at fifteen, she expected her work to be more glamorous and brag-worthy. She spent those warm months sweating through her clothes, feeding animals, and not breathing in too deeply while cleaning out their stalls.

The boots had been tucked away in the back of her closet ever since she moved into her cozy loft apartment. The only reason she hadn't thrown them out was because Mom had gifted them to her as a birthday gift. When her mom moved to Austin once she graduated high school and left for college, the boots felt like a way to keep her close by.

The idea of baling hay didn't excite her. She wasn't sure what there would even be for her to do, other than stay out of the way. She couldn't fathom taking pictures of such a normal ranching task, no matter what Brantley thought. What excitement or emotion was there to capture with something so routine? But she was going regardless. Might as well dress the part.

Milo let out a bark when her phone rang. She glanced at her clock. "I still have twenty minutes," she muttered, feeling unusually rushed this morning. She wasn't used to having breakfast guests, and as nice as having company had been, it threw off her entire Monday morning routine.

"Jillian, why didn't you call me?"

"Hi, Mom." She shimmied on her second boot, but it didn't slide on as smoothly as the first. Without much room to regain her balance, she fell onto the pull-out couch that was her bed. Milo jumped up, tail wagging.

"Your father's in town?"

"Yes. With Stella."

"Are you sure you have the right man?"

Jillian let out a tiny laugh. Years later, they could

finally find humor in being abandoned. "I'm as surprised as you are."

"So it's true, then? They've moved up the wedding?"

"And relocated." She catapulted herself up from the low-lying mattress. Her tiny loft apartment was cramped to say the least. Hardly two-hundred and fifty square feet if one added in the bathroom. But she found enough real estate to hop around on one foot, determined to get this second boot on the rest of the way. Milo quirked his head at her odd bouncing.

"Oh, dear."

"I really wish I didn't have to go." With her mom, she could be honest and not risk hurting anyone's feelings.

"I know. But he's your dad."

She sighed. "I know, I know. It's just that woman . . . She makes me so crazy! And I've only spent an hour with her so far this time. I don't know how I'm going to survive an entire wedding week."

"You sound like you need backup."

She almost told her mom that she had Brantley. But lying to one parent about a fake relationship was enough. Her parents hadn't spoken to each other since she graduated high school. She doubted they'd start now, especially with her mom living in Texas. "I'll be okay, Mom. No need to waste a trip on this disaster." The second boot finally slid onto her foot. "Save your vacation time for something enjoyable."

Her phone buzzed in her hand. Another incoming text.

Future Stepmonster: If you change your mind, manis @ 1. My treat :) I want to hear ALL about that hunky man of yours. XOXO

She fell into a chair with a groan. It was one thing to tolerate Stella's presence in order to see her dad. It was quite another for the woman to presume she wanted to spend one-on-one time together.

"Are you sure?" Mom asked. "You don't sound okay."

Her phone buzzed again.

Brantley: here

"I'm fine, Mom. It's only a few days. I can handle the stepmonster. Gotta go! Love you, bye." She hung up before her mom could pry further.

With all the buzzing from her phone over-whelming her this morning, the temptation to leave it plugged in the charger for the day nudged her. But she sighed, knowing a good business owner was always available for clients, however rare they may be. She couldn't afford to make any bad impressions.

Once downstairs in the studio, she turned to her dog. "Will you be a good boy, Milo?" She couldn't tell him that Holly would be picking him up for a play date with his brother. Milo would whine and pace as if the play date were now. Instead, she dug three of his favorite treats from the cupboard that shared its space with extra camera batteries and tossed them his way. "I'll be back soon. Be a good boy." She pointed at him. "No funny business!"

With the treats to distract him, her dog didn't even lift his head when she slipped out the door. But he did appear in the window, curtains shoved aside, when she got into Brantley's Jeep.

"There's no coffee." She turned sharply to Brantley, but he faced away as he waved to a ranch hand on a four-wheeler. "You said there'd be coffee."

"And there will be, at the ranch. I promise, it's good."

She couldn't fathom what a bunch of ranchers drank for coffee, but she couldn't envision them adding in flavored creamers. She'd go without before she drank it black. "I hope you're right." She set her purse in her lap and hugged it to her chest.

"Everything Violet Livingston touches tastes like magic. Trust me."

"Well, that might persuade me." She had sampled Violet's blue-ribbon pies at the town festival last summer and been scolded for swiping too many samples.

"Got your camera?" he asked.

"I'm not going to need it."

Brantley sat in idle outside her cabin. "That doesn't answer my question."

"I always have my camera."

"Good." He shifted into gear and rolled forward. "How did your class go last night?" Though Brantley had dropped her off, he hadn't stuck around to see the class in action.

A small smile formed on her lips at the memory of Lina Holbrook's face beaming with pride at her first successful selfie. That particular lesson hadn't been on her prepared smartphone photo class syllabus, but she'd hardly been able to tell the dear old woman no. "It went pretty well, I think."

"First time teaching it?" he asked, genuine curiosity in his tone as they left the Maxwell Ranch and headed toward town.

"Yeah." First time teaching anything. She found she rather enjoyed it, but something kept her from saying so. She didn't know any other successful photographers who taught classes like that, but she was trying everything she could to get her name around town. "Teaching a Part Two in a couple of weeks. Lina talked me into it when she drove me home."

"That's great, Jilly." He flashed her a proud smile. "I'm really happy for you."

They meandered through a familiar neighborhood on their way across town. She considered asking him to take another route. She'd grown up on this street and didn't think she could handle seeing her childhood home occupied by someone else. She'd only made the mistake of driving by once since returning after college. It broke her heart.

"Looks like Hudson's sister got hold of that corner house." He pointed to a small square house.

She stared in disbelief at a corner house with its pale blue siding, trimmed hedges, and fresh shingles. She hardly recognized it. Years ago, it'd been in disrepair with its overgrown landscaping suffocating the neglected home's peeling paint. She remembered it from her teenage years, as it had been the eyesore out her bedroom window. "I really thought they'd bulldoze that one."

"Me, too," he said.

"Ronnie's sure been good for Starlight." Ronnie Ross, once a minor but popular character on an interior design reality show, now had her own show in Starlight. Her projects had grown in scale from renovating rooms to now flipping houses.

"That one's for sale," he said. "But I don't think it'd qualify for the show. Looks like it's been kept up a little better."

"Which one?"

He pointed across the dashboard to a split-level house with a screened-in porch. "Didn't you used to live there?"

Her heart dropped. "For sale?" The words hardly escaped as a whisper. She hugged her purse tighter against her chest. "Stop."

"But—"

"Please."

He did as she asked and came to a stop along the curb.

"I grew up here." Whoever had lived here last was gone. Curtains no longer hung in the windows, giving her a clear view through the vacant interior and into the kitchen at the back of the house. How many dinners had they eaten at the island before Dad left? They'd laughed so much back then.

"Hey, you okay?"

A tear escaped, despite her best efforts. She let it fall, wishing for once she'd let her hair down to curtain its path down her cheek. "Yeah."

A warm hand cupped her shoulder, a tingle traveling through her arm at his touch. "Jilly—"

Checking her phone, she pulled up an email from the local real estate agency she took photos for. It confirmed her worst fear. "I'm supposed to shoot pictures here this afternoon. I don't know how I didn't recognize the address."

"I'm sure they can find someone else to do it."

"Let's go. Please." She clamped her eyes shut until she felt the Jeep's sway as he turned a corner.

They drove along the outskirts of town, Brantley now avoiding neighborhoods, until they hit gravel. She was grateful for the silence to regain her composure. That house had once represented a happy, complete family. Her dad spent days working at one ranch or another, her mom taught at the local elementary school, and in the evenings they ate together. Watched TV together. Laughed together.

Now he was in town to marry some other woman. If only she had RSVP'd yes to their original plans, she'd have been spared the salt rubbed into the wound that came with Rodney Harper returning to Starlight.

They continued their journey down the gravel road. "Am I supposed to take pictures all day?" she asked as they crested the hill that revealed the expansive Livingston Ranch, happy to push away any thoughts of that old house and the broken family it now represented. Two tractors puttered through one field, dragging some contraption behind them, turning hay that had already been cut. She'd asked before, but she really hoped Brantley had a better answer this time.

"I'll leave that to Violet."

"But—"

"Unless you're dying to do girly things with Stella." Brantley winked at her.

"Not funny!"

He parked near a cluster of pickups. In all the years she'd lived in Starlight, she had never been to the Livingston Ranch. The main house stretched a great distance, and a handful of people sat scattered on the covered porch. She counted half a dozen cabins in a circle off in one direction, a couple of two-story barns in another.

She hopped out of the truck, feeling out of place. She'd only worked on a ranch those summers as a teen. And she couldn't recall being very good at it. Taking care of the horses for Holly was a simple chore, but anything beyond that . . . A tractor roared, passing by them on the graveled drive. Someone waved, but she couldn't tell who. "I hope no one expects me to drive one of those."

"Of course not, dear." The voice, too feminine to be Brantley, startled her. Violet Livingston appeared from behind the truck, a sunflower-patterned apron hiding a pair of jeans and work boots. "The men will handle all of that. They like that sort of thing. Unless you want someone to teach you?"

She shook her head. Halfway around the truck, Brantley was intercepted by a couple of the ranch hands. "I hope I won't be in the way . . ."

"Don't you worry about that. Are you two here all day?"

The words *you two* struck an odd chord. One night out for dinner and now this? Had the rumor about their supposed relationship spread to the Livingston Ranch? Would everyone here think they were a couple, or would they simply see through the lie and blow her cover?

"Probably not. I have a house to shoot this afternoon." But already she was tempted to take Brantley's advice and request they find another photographer. The mere hundred and fifty dollars she'd earn for that shoot didn't seem worth the torment being back in that home might cause.

She watched Brantley clap a ranch hand on the shoulder before rounding the back of the truck. He gave Violet a squeeze. "We get any of that famous pie today?"

Eyes twinkling, Violet rubbed her hands against her apron. "You know I made a few. You boys are never happy with one slice."

"You're the best, Violet." Brantley shoved his hands into his front pockets. "Hope you don't mind, thought maybe Jillian could grab some pictures throughout the day."

"That would be lovely!" Violet beamed at the idea. "I'll have Jed grab you a four-wheeler." Violet zipped off before she could ask why she'd need one. Brantley kicked at the gravel beneath his boots.

"You're really stuck on this idea of me taking pictures," she said with folded arms. "What am I supposed to take pictures *of*?" She tried to keep her voice low, but she drew attention anyway. Too many people lingered. She never imagined wielding a camera for something so common. She wanted to photograph the special occasions in people's lives when the emotions were at their height. She wasn't sure what emotions could be captured during routine hay baling.

"Today. This."

She closed her eyes to imagine other ways to avoid her overbearing future stepmom. Maybe a road trip to Gillette? Or hiding out at Holly's house for the day? Lost in her thoughts, she was caught off guard when Brantley draped an arm on her shoulders and led her away from the porch, out onto the open driveway.

"Over there." He pointed to the two tractors she'd observed earlier. "They're turning hay. It was cut a couple days ago but needed time to dry. That pasture won't be ready to bale for a couple of days yet, if the weather cooperates."

"What—"

"Shh. Listen." He turned her toward another pasture, his arm warm against her shoulders and across her back. She shook away any thoughts about Brantley's touch that dared trespass in her mind. Out here, they didn't have to pretend. "That pasture over there is one they'll bale today. Take the camera. Don't get in their way but do what you do best. Capture the essence of the day."

Her heart rate ticked up. Was that a compliment? "But—"

Someone called for Brantley, and he dropped his arm and put a step of space between them, as if he'd been caught doing something wrong. "Hope you brought a spare battery for that camera. I think you'll be surprised what you capture." He hurried away, toward the ranch hand who called him over, leaving her on her own.

"Ma'am." Her attention turned toward a young man, probably fifteen or sixteen by her best judgment. "You ever driven a four-wheeler?"

$\mathcal{B}$rantley

Bringing Jillian along for the day might've been one of his worst ideas yet. He hadn't counted on being so distracted by her in those cowgirl boots. He hadn't seen her wear those in years.

She'd done a great job already, staying off to the side while remaining close to the action. Hopefully she managed some good shots. He wanted her to see for herself that opportunity existed outside of real estate photos and weddings.

"She just needs a nudge," Edie told him the last time Jillian came up in conversation. "So give her one."

When the opportunity presented itself, he did just that. Jillian'd been stuck in a box he didn't know how to talk her out of when it came to the success of her studio. He wanted to see her business grow.

"You good, man?" Hudson wiped away a line of sweat on his forehead with the back of his hand.

He again had been caught watching Jillian up on the trailer, currently lying stomach down on a pile of hay bales, snapping photos. Even that pesky messy bun had him daydreaming about loosening her hair tie and letting those long locks of auburn hair fall against her shoulders in the sunlight.

"Yeah, I'm good." Someone had apparently found her a blanket. He couldn't imagine her tolerating scratchy hay all day.

"Heard Corrine tried to take you home the other night."

That was the one thing he would never get used to in his small hometown. Not only how quickly rumors spread, but the way they got twisted. "She wanted me to have a drink with her. Which I didn't." He hoped that particular rumor wouldn't float its way to Jillian's dad.

Or worse, Stella.

"But you bought her a drink."

He pulled off his hat and raked a hand through his hair. "Figured it was the easiest way to escape." Now he wasn't so sure.

"You don't escape from Corrine Daily when she has her sights set. She likes a challenge."

"Speaking from experience?"

Hudson tossed a hay bale onto the trailer. "Be careful. That kind of persistence can cause complications." He marched off after the next bale a dozen yards away, leaving Brantley with a cold shiver.

———

"We headed to that place you need to shoot?" he asked as they drove away from the Livingston Ranch a few hours later. He was careful not to specifically mention, *childhood home*. Jillian seemed happy throughout the day, but she hadn't mentioned that house once.

"I rescheduled."

He rolled to a stop at the first stop sign back into Starlight, waiting on an approaching truck. The sun aimed its glaring beam right at his eyes, forcing him to pull down the sun visor. "Could they get someone else?" Rescheduled simply meant she put it off, and he suspected she'd only put it off again.

She shrugged, a stray wavy hair falling against her cheek. "I asked but no one else can do it." Such nonchalance in her voice, as if the house no longer held its emotional grip on her heart. But he didn't buy it.

"Jilly—"

"I'd kill someone for a cheeseburger right now."

Relenting, he turned instead of going straight. "Mabel's Diner it is."

He wasn't ready to take her home anyway, and Holly would keep Milo as long as needed; she'd sent him a text a couple of hours ago saying as much. He'd never told Holly how he felt about Jillian, but his cousin was perceptive enough to figure it out. He would bet his Jeep on it.

Jillian ordered a bacon cheeseburger with a side of fries she promised to share, as he didn't have much of an appetite. "Filled up on Violet's pie," he lied. Violet had given out apple, peach, and blueberry pies today. He even had a whole one in the back seat of his Jeep.

But it was untouched.

"Today was fun." Jillian twirled a straw around the rim of her lemonade glass.

She looked adorable, elbows perched on the table, a couple rebel locks of hair dangling beside one cheek as she looked over the dessert menu. He yearned to brush those stray auburn locks of hair behind her ear, but it was too risky without a reason to act like a couple. No Rodney or Stella in sight to provide cover for such an action in public.

"Did you get a lot of pictures?"

"Way more than I should have." Her green eyes sparkled as she slipped the dessert menu back behind the ketchup and mustard. "I can't wait to get back to the studio and edit them. Like the one of Hudson on the tractor." She rambled halfway through the plate of fries, her burger hardly touched with her excitement pouring out about the shots she captured. "I'm going to print a few and give them to Violet as a gift."

"I think that's a great idea."

As Jillian finally reached for her burger, her phone buzzed on the table. One look at that happy expression turned sour, and even before he saw Jillian's nickname for Stella—Future Stepmonster—on her screen, he knew it could only be one person. "Ugh!"

"What is it with you and Stella?" he asked, stealing a fry from her plate. "Have you two ever gotten along?"

"Not really." She slid her phone into her purse and dipped a fry in her honey mustard, causing him to cringe a little. "Lots of people dip their fries in honey mustard, Brantley." A cute smile crossed her lips before she took a bite, but it wasn't the same smile as before.

The server brought them drink refills. Jillian probably knew the woman, as she picked up odd shifts here at the diner. But he rarely stopped unless he spotted Jillian's car in the back lot. He wasn't much for diner food.

"Dad asked me to come visit about a year ago."

Jillian stared at her plate, pushing fries around with another fry. "But he didn't warn me."

"About Stella?"

"That he'd been seeing anyone at all."

"Oh."

"Imagine my surprise when I showed up at his doorstep and a stranger answered the door, wearing a blinding diamond on a certain ring finger."

"No."

She stabbed a fry into her honey mustard. "Oh, yes."

He wanted to comfort her in some way. Hold her hand or graze her arm with his fingertips. Instead, he balled up his napkin beneath the table.

"She had the nerve to greet me as my *new mom*." She finally took a bite of her neglected burger, savoring it if her closed eyes were any indication. "My dad had run to the store to pick up some steaks, so I had an entire precious hour with Stella hovering. Guess she wanted to make sure I actually unpacked my bags and didn't run."

He waved down the server for the check. "Was this the first woman your dad dated?" *Since he left.* But he didn't say that part out loud. He remembered how awful that summer was for Jillian, despite her best efforts at hiding her pain from the world. More than once, he came across her hiding in an empty horse stall, cheeks puffy and eyes glistening.

"It's not like I held out some hope that my parents would get back together. They were all wrong for each other. I see that now." She dabbed a napkin at the barbeque sauce on the corner of her mouth. He had to look away or thoughts of kissing her there would haunt him all night long. "He dated. But yes, this was the first one I knew about. Certainly the first one I met."

"What a way to find out."

"No kidding." She dropped her napkin on her plate and pushed it to the edge of the table. "From the first, she had an opinion about everything. I know you think I'm exaggerating, but I'm not. She had to comment about my flip-flops. How it looked like I could use a new pair, and we could go shopping together."

He had to play devil's advocate a little bit. Though he had a full dose of Stella last night, she could be misunderstood. Either way, it seemed as though her dad was going through with the wedding. If he could help Jillian discover some redeeming quality about her future stepmother, he would. "She only wanted to bond."

"They were brand new sandals. I bought them that morning on my way to the airport."

He slipped the server some cash with the ticket and scooted back from his chair. "Then, maybe she wanted an excuse to shop."

"It's not like it stopped there." Jillian slung her

purse over her shoulder and followed him back to the Jeep. "You know how she brought up my studio?"

"How?" He opened her door, mostly because he could. Jillian seemed oblivious to any gesture he made right now. Maybe another man would be discouraged, but he hoped she'd find herself missing this extra attention come next week.

"She said, and I quote, 'I heard you take pictures. What an adorable *hobby*.'" She huffed her way into the passenger seat. "I'd literally opened my studio three weeks prior. Told my dad all about the grand opening."

Letting the door close, he slowly rounded his Jeep. The pieces were falling together. The timing. Her fiancé dumped her on opening day. Then a short time later, she learned her dad was getting married to a woman she'd never even heard a peep about. *Jilly.*

"I know you probably think I was a brat the whole time I was there. And believe me, I wanted to be," she continued when he got in. "But I tried to be the understanding daughter, because my dad seemed happy. I even offered to take engagement photos."

Oh, no.

"Stella waved away my offer and said not to worry. She'd hire a *professional*." He could nearly see steam floating from her ears. Her cheeks gleamed red in the light of the setting sun.

"That's . . . Jilly, I'm . . ." But he didn't have words to make things better.

"She did it again when I offered to take wedding photos."

If he had entertained thoughts about bailing on their fake relationship agreement, he pushed them away now. He wouldn't force her to face this wedding without him. At least he could deflect the brunt of it all.

"That was when I exaggerated my success a little bit. During that visit. Because the truth wasn't good enough, and Stella kept prodding me." Jillian let out a long yawn. "I know, I know. I should've taken the high road and been honest. I wouldn't be in this mess at all if I had. But now I don't want to make my dad look a fool for believing me."

"You're in a tight spot." They rolled onto the graveled entrance to the Maxwell Ranch, dipping below the large arch made of old telephone poles with a laser-cut sign displaying the name. A creation Holly came up with.

"It's only five more days, right?"

"Right."

Too soon, they were outside Jillian's cabin. Milo's head poked up in the window. Brantley'd sent Holly a text when they left the diner, asking her to bring the pup back. He hadn't wanted Jillian driving across the ranch to pick him up after the long day she had in the sun.

"See you at seven?"

Her jaw fell open. "In the morning?"

Unable to resist, he lifted her chin with his index finger to push it closed. "Breakfast all week, remember? It was such a great suggestion." He let his finger slide slowly from her smooth skin, wishing he was drawing her in for a kiss instead.

CHAPTER 9

illian

Tuesday and Thursday mornings, Jillian fed and watered the horses on the ranch. It was her arrangement with the Maxwell family for utilizing the cabin as both her photography studio and living quarters. One her best friend-slash-ranch manager orchestrated back when Jillian decided to follow through with her dream to open a studio a little more than a year ago.

"Hey there, Lucy." She greeted her favorite strawberry roan mare. On cue, the horse turned her muzzle and let her rub the soft coat with her palm. "Don't tell anyone, but I brought you an apple."

She was only afraid of horses when it came to the idea of riding one again. As long as she had both feet firmly planted on the ground, everything was okay.

It'd been a crazy set of circumstances, really. She'd been helping Holly exercise a couple of the horses on a trail they both knew well. She'd ridden Timmy, a young horse that tended to fall asleep halfway through their ride, many times.

Jillian refilled water for the horses, one by one.

Timmy'd been dozing off when a rabbit skittered across their path, pursued by a fox, and, more startled than anything, the horse bucked. She didn't have a proper grip on the reins, much less the saddle, and she flew backward and smacked her side into a tree with rather scratchy bark—a tree almost fifteen feet from where she'd been astride only seconds before.

Every time she considered getting back on a horse, it was that detail that bothered her most. Not that a horse *could* buck her, but that one could throw her *so far*. Because if Timmy had been turned a little more to the right, he would have bucked her right down the side of a steep and very rocky cliff. All in all, she felt lucky she hadn't gotten a concussion. But she had nightmares about that cliff for a long time after the accident.

"I saw you give her that apple." Brantley's voice echoed in the high-ceilinged stable. "Lucy'll keep your secret, but I might have to be bribed."

She normally wasn't rattled at all by his presence. He often stopped by on the mornings she had chores. But today, her pulse seemed to jump to a light sprint. She'd tried to avoid him by leaving a plate of muffins and a fresh glass of orange juice on the porch with a note. "Lucy wouldn't forgive you if you did." She tried to meet his eyes, but after last night, she kept her gaze trained on the stall gate over his shoulder. Had he wanted to *kiss* her when he dropped her off?

"Lucy likes me too much to stay mad." The air between them was charged as Brantley sauntered her way. It shouldn't be charged. Jillian shuffled back a couple of steps, kicking over a bucket in the process. Her phone pinged, but she ignored it. Likely Stella again.

The more frightening thought was that *she* might have wanted him to kiss her.

She picked up the bucket, but the way to the hose was around Brantley. And he didn't seem interested in making her escape easy. He was enjoying this, if the smirk on his face was any indication.

"Can I get by?" Why did the words sound weak and small?

He stepped back. "By all means." The wafting of his cologne settled in a cloud around her, causing her to scurry even faster to the water pump outside the stable.

Another ping.

Almost a year ago, Brantley used to stop by her studio every day, always with an excuse to check on this or fix that. They'd started eating lunches together. He took an interest in her photos, even the boring ones. She'd started dreaming about him. Found herself wanting to kiss him.

The day she decided to be brave, to kiss him and see what happened, she never got the chance. There on her front porch, on his way to have lunch with her, he got the worst call of his life. If she had ever needed a sign, that was it. They had a friendship she would cross oceans to protect. That one kiss might've ruined it all.

She let the loud splash of the water against the metal of the bucket drown out all hints of him. Except that she could feel his eyes burning a hole through the back of her shirt.

"You go through any of those photos yet?"

"Only a few so far." She had to shuffle around him to empty her bucket into the trough. Her phone pinged three times in quick succession. "Hoping to go through the rest later this morning."

"You'll have to let me see how they turned out."

She raised an eyebrow at him. "Trying to get lunch out of me too, now?"

"Well, if you're offering . . ."

Half a dozen pings sounded, and she couldn't take it anymore. She dropped the bucket, water splashing over the rim and onto the hay. "I swear, this better be an emergency. If someone isn't dying . . ." She scrolled through the notifications. One from her dad. Thirteen from Stella.

"Everything okay?"

"She's crazy, Brantley. Absolutely out of her mind."

He was closer somehow. She hadn't seen him move, and with the sun pouring into the stable, his shadow should've caught her attention when it moved. She was a little unsettled by his stealth, but not as unsettled as she was from Stella's texts.

"So?"

"Well, no one's dead or even injured."

"What a letdown."

"Right? There should at least be a broken bone." She let out a heavy sigh, enough to catch Lucy's attention. The mare reached her nose over the stall gate and nudged her ear. She rested her head a moment against Lucy. "She wants me to meet her at the hotel. Something about pedicures, dress fittings, and Holly."

"Holly?"

She shrugged. "She says bring a girlfriend. Holly's the only one I have. I don't know why, though."

"You going?"

The horses were fed, watered, and brushed.

Stalls cleaned, fresh hay delivered. She wanted to say no. Wanted to pretend her phone had been lost in a river and she never received the texts. Her phone pinged again.

Future Stepmonster: I can bring the dresses to you. What's your address?

"Looks like going is my wisest choice."

———

Before a hit reality show came to town last summer, Starlight had been a little lacking in overnight accommodations. There was the Sleepy Starlight Motel on the outskirts of town, desperately in need of a paint job and someone to pull weeds. And a couple of basic chain hotels had nestled their way in, closer to downtown along the main drag.

But with the popularity of the town growing via reality TV fame, a developer had snatched up a vacant plot of land and built a lavish resort.

"You owe me lunch for this." Holly pushed the passenger car door open and hopped out before she could express her gratitude. Convincing her to abandon a desk full of books and receipts already a couple of days behind hadn't been easy. "I thought Brantley was supposed to be attached to your hip this week?" Holly added before she closed the car door.

Jillian cut the engine. She squeezed the straps of her purse and forced herself out of the car. "Stella insisted it had to be a girl I brought along." This was a mess. A big, giant mess. "Let's be quick, and I'll buy you lunch. Anything you want."

"I want a steak." Holly tossed her a cheesy smile.

But when she tried to return the gesture, her expression wouldn't quite cooperate. If she'd only agreed to go to the stupid wedding in Cancun, none of this would be happening. Her dad and future stepmonster wouldn't be in *her* town. Her less than fabulous life wouldn't be on the brink of being uncovered.

Not the first time she'd scolded herself about this. But now there was also the thought that Brantley wouldn't have to pretend to be her boyfriend. There'd be no more confusing thoughts about wanting or not wanting to kiss him swirling in her head.

"I'm sorry she's dragging you into all this," she said at the revolving door, waiting for an empty space to hop into. "But I'd be lying if I said I wasn't grateful you're here to keep me in check. I don't know what my dad sees in her, but I'm not trying to ruin his wedding."

They stepped out into the lavish lobby, and for a moment, both women were struck with the excessive luxury. The high ceilings, the gigantic chandelier that looked more suited to an opera house, the marble floors. Exactly the kind of thing Stella loved.

"There you girls are!" Stella's booming voice echoed off the high ceilings as her heeled stride clacked across the marble floor. "Come, come. It's time for pedicures at their spa!"

"Stella, we really don't have time—"

Stella latched onto Jillian's arm and tugged. "They're on me."

Jillian looked at Holly, who shrugged.

So much for being in and out. She should have known better when it came to a quick favor from Stella. It should also come as no surprise that this excessive resort had a spa. She tried not to calculate what these pedicures would cost her dad.

Pastel blue walls and white string lights lined a private room with three chairs. Water already bubbled at the foot of each.

"Are those oranges?" Holly asked at the foot of the first chair, her head tilted to get a better look.

"Orange peel pedicures." Stella kicked off her high-heeled sandals and sank into the middle chair. "They're the best!"

Jillian offered a pitiful look as apology and let Holly have the chair closest to the exit. If only one of them could escape, it should be her best friend who had graciously agreed to sacrifice her morning.

Three technicians entered the room, each offering the women beverages, some with umbrellas. At least a fruity, if overpriced, mimosa would help keep her from winding up tight. She took an eager sip as a woman got to work on her feet. For a moment, she simply sank back into the cushy massage chair, closed her eyes, and drifted off.

Until Stella's booming voice interrupted.

"I need another bridesmaid. I had a last-minute cancellation. You don't mind, do you Holl?"

"Um . . ."

Jillian cringed. Of course there was a reason Stella wanted a *girlfriend* to join them this morning. If only she'd thought it through, she might've thought to warn her best friend. Or not bring her at all. "Stella, I think Holly might be tied up with running a ranch—"

"I would be forever grateful." Stella batted her eyelashes, which oddly enough worked to elicit the sympathy. "My cousin Betty can't make it, but without another bridesmaid it'll totally throw off the balance of the ceremony. Not to mention the head table!"

The technician took that awkward moment to rub the dead skin off the bottom of Jillian's feet, which caused her to squeal and squirm. "Sorry!" It was inconvenient to have to bite down on your lip when all you wanted to do was save your best friend.

"Think of how much fun it'll be if *both* you and Jillian are in the wedding!"

Jillian watched Holly's wide eyes return back to their normal size. "It could be fun," she mused, swirling her free foot in the bubbly, blue-tinted water.

"Holly, you don't—" Another squeal. She really hated how ticklish she was. Her technician was completely unaffected by her outburst and merely tightened her grip on her foot.

"There'll be single men your age there."

"What?" She couldn't fathom who they'd be. Both Stella and her dad were well into their late fifties. Well, there was Stella's annoying nephew, Chad. Judging by the devious twinkle in her future stepmonster's eyes, that might be exactly what she was up to.

"Well, not for *you,* Jill. Not with your hunky boyfriend and all." Stella assessed her with an intent look, completely unaffected by the buffer being wielded beneath her foot like a table saw. "Unless it's not that serious."

"Oh, it is," Holly chimed in.

"Yeah," Jillian agreed. Because what else could she do? "Two years and all."

Stella squinted her eyes, leaning toward her. "Why aren't you wearing a ring?" she asked, as nonchalantly as one might ask what she had for lunch. "Surely if it was serious, he'd have popped the question by now."

Jillian sucked in a breath so deep air shoved its way clear to her toes; she counted to five. "We're not in a hurry."

"Oh, dear." Stella *tsk*ed, shaking her head.

With her face so closely pointed in Jillian's direction, it was impossible not to notice the inordinate amount of eye makeup she wore. The thick black eyeliner in a perfect curled shape. The mixture of blues and teals of her eye shadow. On anyone else it might've looked tacky, but Stella somehow pulled it off. *Amazing.*

"They've known each other since they were teenagers," Holly said, calm as ever. She didn't show an ounce of the panic Jillian felt bubbling inside her chest. It was one thing to be untruthful over the phone, but quite another to lie in person like this. She might blow the whole thing with one wrong facial expression.

"So what's taking so long?" Stella asked. "Have you been leaving hints?"

"No . . ."

"Are you sure? That could be driving him away if you're not subtle enough. I've mastered it by now, but it took three husbands to get me there. Maybe he's not the marrying type?"

"Brantley's really a great guy," Holly said.

"Patient, hardworking, kind-hearted. Perfect for Jillian, really."

Jillian tried to meet her best friend's gaze over Stella's busty chest, but Holly's eyes were averted. The words . . . they sounded almost genuine. But Holly knew it was simply a fake relationship. She suggested it. Come next week, things would go back to the way they were.

"Maybe *you're* not the marrying type?" Such innocence seemed to linger in those words, swirling over the pedicurist's head. But she felt the stab anyway. She felt that way when her fiancé showed up at her grand opening and demanded she give him her ring back. "It's nothing to be ashamed of," Stella went on. "Some folks aren't cut out for it."

"Where are you having the wedding?" Holly asked. Later, she would hug her friend so tight, squeezing all the air completely out of her lungs.

"Why, right here at the hotel, of course. They have an amazing ballroom." Stella rambled on about the accommodations, the décor, the food. But she heard little of it.

You're not the marrying type . . . Stella's words had touched a nerve, whether the woman had intended them to or not. What if she was right? What if the real reason her ex left was because she wasn't the type of girl a man married? It shouldn't bother her so much, considering she'd been single since his departure.

Stella turned toward her. "The seamstress just arrived. She'll be up in our suite. Need you both to try on your dresses." She looked Holly up and down the best she could from her pedicure recliner. "Yours will need a bit of altering. I'm afraid my cousin Betty is a bit bustier than you."

Jillian met Holly's gaze—*five days*.

"Why don't I meet you girls upstairs? Room 312." Stella pushed out of her chair, walking on her heels in the flat foam sandals they'd slipped on her feet. "One of you be a doll and bring my shoes when you're done?"

She and Holly shared a second-long look that spoke volumes. Their friendship had always included that perk. They somehow knew how to say everything without uttering a single word.

"Holly, I'm sorry she sabotaged you," she said once the technicians moved them to the drying table and walked out of earshot. "I had no idea she was going to ask you to be in the wedding. I thought she wanted you there to help me get into a dress."

"Sometimes you just have to go with the flow, right?"

"You're the most amazing best friend a girl could have."

Holly pasted on a cheesy smile, eyes twinkling mischievously. "I know."

"I should've gone to Cancun."

Bumping her with her elbow, Holly reminded, "She's wrong, you know."

"About what?"

"Jason wasn't the marrying type. Not you." Holly pushed back out of her chair and slipped back into her sandals. "Let's go see what kind of knockouts we're going to be in these bridesmaids' dresses!"

CHAPTER 10

*B**rantley***

During any normal week, Brantley would never have time for a spontaneous hike with his fake girlfriend and her family. He had responsibilities at the ranch. After Paul passed away, he made Holly promise to keep him as busy as possible. As the ranch manager, she was in charge of the schedule. She consulted with a lead ranch hand about how to divvy out those tasks, but she was the one who gave the final approval.

So it only made sense that his cousin was up to something. Because his name wasn't even *on* the schedule today.

"I don't know why we have to meet them at Trey's," Jillian mumbled once the Jeep was parked.

Milo paced in the back seat, excited to be on an adventure. Sometimes he wished he could be happy as easily as a dog seemed to. What did Milo have to worry about other than the occasional squirrel and who would share their pizza with him?

"Probably wanted to pick up some bug spray before we hit the trail."

Jillian rubbed Milo behind the ears. "Suppose we better go in, huh?" The excitement in her voice rivaled that of someone about to walk on hot coals.

"Suppose so."

Trey's Outfitters was the only outdoor store for fifty miles or more. Cool air washed over them inside the second set of automatic sliding doors. A display rack of women's camo clothing with clearance signs stood right up front. Trey's was smaller than most, but he had the same high ceilings and log home interior feeling of a chain store. He stocked a variety of items from kayaks to fishing poles to apparel for any outdoor activity imaginable.

"There you two lovebirds are!" Stella's voice trilled, echoing off the high ceilings and turning all attention to him and Jillian. He slipped his arm around her and ushered them both to Stella, already at the checkout counter with a pile of finds.

"So much for browsing," Jillian mumbled.

"You mean procrastinating," he said right up against her ear. He told himself he did it because Stella was watching. "Looks like you picked out a few things, Stella." He nodded at the mound of clothes on the counter, because Jillian seemed unusually quiet. She hadn't told him much about the morning pedicures. He scanned the store, but didn't see any sign of Rodney.

"The hotel recommended we get better gear. Said Trey's was the best place in town." The cashier had only begun the process of scanning and folding all the clothes. They'd be waiting a few minutes.

It was reassuring that the new chain hotel was recommending local businesses. Plenty of locals feared people would forego the local shops in favor of bigger chains in Gillette. Or worse, open their own outdoor stores within the hotel walls. Trey's had anything one could want when it came to outdoor adventures.

"It's a short hike, right?" Jillian asked. "I have some photos to edit tonight." Which he instantly translated as she had a shift at the diner and didn't want to be late. They were hard enough to come by, she had told him just last week. Being late could mean it was her last shift.

"Two hours tops," Stella answered.

"Where's Dad?"

Stella nodded toward the corner of the store that showcased tents, a slight roll of her eyes following. "He heard something about a rooftop tent and had to see it for himself. Honestly, I don't know what the man would do with camping gear. It was all I could do to get him on this little hike."

"Rooftop tent?"

"Yeah, something you can mount on top of a car or truck. Completely ridiculous if you ask me. All the best places have lodges. No sense in sleeping in a tent if you have a perfectly good shower and cushy mattress, I always say." Stella reached into her shirt to pluck out her cell phone; he wished he'd looked away sooner. "Brantley, would you be a dear and fetch Rodney? We need to meet the trail guide."

He tried to meet Jillian's eyes, seeking permission. Without knowing what transpired that morning, he wasn't eager to leave her unattended with Stella. But without an excuse to stay by her side, he relented. "I'll get him."

Rodney stood with folded arms, admiring the black and gray rooftop tent mounted atop a fake 4Runner. At its height, it appeared at least three and a half feet. Not enough room to stand, but definitely enough for one to kneel. Trey, the store owner, was animated as ever as he described its many features.

"Brantley," Rodney said, a possible smile on his face. At least he thought it was for him. Could be the prospect of owning a rooftop tent. "Check this out." He nodded.

"You in the market?" Trey shook Brantley's hand.

"Nah. Don't know what I'd do with one."

"Travel more," Trey suggested, adding an easy laugh that he and Rodney joined in on.

"There's that." But he didn't do much of that. He was a homebody, always had been even when he was in the military. He was stationed in Alaska, and if it weren't for the luck of ending up in the same unit as his brother and Paul's best friend Mason, he might've stayed right on Fort Wainwright and never ventured outside the base his whole time there.

"You check this out?" Rodney asked him. "It mounts flat on the top of your vehicle. Then when you're ready to set up camp for the night, you push a button. The whole thing sets itself up. Little ladder comes down. Show him, Trey."

He couldn't deny the unique tent had him intrigued. He thought Paul might've mentioned one for their trip, but he wasn't sure. They'd planned to camp, certainly. Much cheaper than motel or lodge rooms.

Trey worked a remote that fit into the palm of his hand, and the tent flattened.

"Think of all the places you could go," said Rodney, a dangerous gleam in his eyes. One that suggested he was about to make a purchase his future wife wouldn't be too pleased about. "You'd never have to worry about making reservations. You could wake up with the sunrise."

Briefly, the idea to buy the rooftop tent so he

could finish the trip he'd never gotten to take with Paul swept him away. They'd planned to visit dozens of state and national parks, and camping was the only economical solution to such a plan. A rooftop tent made it almost impossible to argue against going.

Rodney nudged his shoulder. "Tempting, isn't it?"

"A little." Holly could manage without him for a couple of months. They had more than enough help this summer. Bobby was pretty good with a hammer, and there were other handymen she could call up if the need arose for someone more specialized.

"Looks like you're being summoned." Trey nodded toward Jillian and Stella at the front counter. Stella was waving them down as though she were stranded on the side of the road and they were the only car for miles.

But it was the sight of Jillian, hands in the front pockets of her light pink sweatshirt, an annoyed expression on her face, that brought him back to reality. "The women sent me over here to get you." He didn't want to rob Trey of a sale, but he wasn't sure how Rodney would ship that contraption on a plane. Even in its box it was sizable and hefty. "Something about a trail guide."

Rodney's smile dropped. "I don't know whose bright idea it was to go on a hike," he mumbled. "Trey, I expect I'll be back to see you before the week is over."

The thought of leaving Starlight for weeks or months at a time, of leaving Jillian behind . . . he couldn't. It might be different if Paul were still here. The trip was supposed to be theirs together. Without his brother, it seemed foolish to go.

Walking back to the front counter, he looked over his shoulder at the now fully extended tent. Trey was folding the ladder. It would fit perfectly on the top of his Jeep.

"You boys ready for our little hike?" Stella's booming voice brought him back to the present.

He remembered he was supposed to be playing the part of the doting boyfriend and slipped an arm around Jillian's shoulders and pulled her against him. "Ready." He realized he liked the way she fit beneath his arm a little too much to leave Starlight.

And what if this time while he was gone, Jillian actually got married to someone else?

CHAPTER 11

*J*illian

Stella's *little* hike turned out not so little at all. Jillian was sure she'd be late for her shift at Mabel's Diner, the only one she had this week since she had to give up her Saturday shift to make the wedding. Saturday shifts were hard to come by as they usually resulted in the best tips.

"We'll make it." Brantley sped down a back road she'd never been on, his Jeep making quick work of the terrain. Her poor car would never withstand the ruts and choppiness of what looked to be little more than a cattle trail. Milo barked a couple of times from the back, as if to say he was quite enjoying this little off-roading adventure. "It's a shortcut."

In the distance, she watched a herd of cattle munch nonchalantly on the grass, no sense of urgency in a single one of them. "I don't even have time for a shower."

"Sure you do."

"But—"

"I'll take you."

Jillian studied him a moment, but had to look away. The hike hadn't made him look beat up and worse for wear. Not the way it had her with her tangled hair and dirty knees from an encounter with a low branch and a muddy patch of ground. It'd done quite the opposite, and it was annoying. His hair was more unruly than usual, and the dirty smudge on his sleeve from where she grabbed on to him somehow made him more attractive. "Another shortcut?"

"I know all kinds. Jilly, I have a Jeep. You didn't really think I used it for Sunday driving?"

They'd been friends for years. Better friends since he moved back to Starlight when his Army enlistment was up. But she realized how little she seemed to know about him. "You like to go off-roading?"

"On occasion." He locked eyes with hers for a moment and waggled his eyebrows. "You should come with me sometime."

She laughed.

Their friendship had revolved primarily around the location of her studio. Until this whole fake relationship debacle began, she had never even seen the inside of his cabin. She'd gone there once days before he was supposed to leave for basic training, lingered a short distance from the front steps working up her nerve. But then fat raindrops splashed against her arms, and she took the hint to turn around and go home.

"We'll see." She hopped out of the Jeep and sprinted to the door after he promised to see to Milo.

She showered in record time, forced to leave her hair up and unwashed. At least she'd managed to keep the mud out of it. But if she were late for this shift, it might be her last. For as many customers as Mabel charmed, she wasn't too lenient with her employees if they weren't reliable.

At her open front door, Jillian froze, hands braced against the jamb, and watched Brantley and her dog on the porch. Brantley had his arm around Milo, the dog standing in his lap with front paws on Brantley's shoulders. He'd always been good with her dog, she mused. Something she never really noticed or appreciated. Brantley laughed as Milo licked his face.

She slipped the camera from her desk and discreetly snapped a few photos. The light and shadows on the porch were fantastic for a portrait.

Maybe she'd print one as a thank-you gift for him once this week was all over.

She set her camera back on her desk. She hated to interrupt the moment, but she had no choice. "You two about ready?"

"Ready." Brantley hopped up to his feet. "Mr. Milo here watered your flowers."

True to his word, Brantley dropped her off at the diner with three minutes to spare before the start of her shift. "You don't mind keeping Milo?" she asked as the first few raindrops fell. She'd planned to leave him with Holly again, but there wasn't time to drop him off. And with the darkening clouds promising a downpour, she didn't want to burden her bestie with two wet dogs.

Milo popped his head over the center console, and Brantley rubbed his neck. "It's just gonna be two boys hanging out." Milo's bushy tail swished against the leather seat. "Don't worry about us."

"Text me. Let me know if he's misbehaving."

"Go!"

She hurried through the back door, tying on her apron with one minute to spare.

"Wondered if I was going to see you today." Mabel wore a stern scowl she kept hidden from most of her customers. Only those who had worked for the woman would believe it. Starlight loved their friendly diner owner and her special comfort food.

"Got tied up. My Dad—"

"Table twelve just got sat. They need water." With that, Mabel marched off. She reached into her apron pocket for a notepad, double checked that the ink still flowed through her pen, then proceeded to rush around nonstop for nearly six hours.

Jillian's body ached as the end of her shift loomed nearer. What she wouldn't give for a soak in a hot bath. Of course, that would require one to have a bathtub, something her little loft apartment could never accommodate.

The quick hike had been very hilly and filled with sizeable tree roots growing on the dirt path. The trail guide never seemed deterred by any of it, though. He smiled too much, and called everything a wonder of nature.

Even when Jillian tripped on a protruding root and landed on her knees in the soft mud.

"Table six is you, right?" Sasha, one of Mabel's regular waitresses, asked her back in the kitchen. She was waiting for the cook to finish assembling their special Starlight Burger for table twelve.

"Yeah, that's mine."

"Be warned, they're a little high maintenance.

The woman already asked for a cosmo." Sash rolled her eyes.

"Wonderful." Just what she needed at the end of her shift; a customer who was satisfied by nothing the diner had to offer. She wished Mabel were still here to smooth things over. She had some magical spell with peevish customers that always left them happy and satisfied.

"Can I bribe you?" she asked in jest.

"I already had a bad one today. Tipped me with a handful of pennies." Sasha shook her head, her jet-black hair tossing back and forth from her ponytail. "You can't afford to bribe me."

She let out a sigh. With any luck, this would be her last customer of the evening.

"You'll also need to tell them we don't have sparkling water," Sasha added. "I told her I'd check."

"But we never have sparkling—" The horrific possibility that she knew these customers smacked her right in the gut. She craned her neck out the doorway to get a decent look at table six. But it was hard to view from this angle.

"Jillian," the cook said, nodding at two plates of food ready to be delivered. "You gonna take this?"

"Thanks." She grabbed the plates and slipped out into the dining room as a new burger hitting the grill sizzled.

Desperation for invisibility clawed at her. If her

dad and Stella really were at the diner, they couldn't see her like this. They'd never understand. She'd spent the hike telling them about all her clients. Sure, they'd mostly been made-up clients she hoped to gain in the future. But the life she described didn't allow or require things like a periodic waitressing shift.

With skills that could only be compared to a ninja, she managed to deliver two plates to her other customers and a couple of drink refills without drawing the attention of table six, who were indeed her dad and Stella.

She zipped back to the kitchen, searching for Sasha. "I'll pay you to take them."

"I don't know. I might be tempted to trip and spill ice water on that woman. Then Mabel would fire me . . . I don't think it's worth my job."

"How much?" she asked. She hated the idea of giving up any of the tips she'd worked hard to earn today. She needed the money to put toward a new backdrop and frames for a couple of the Livingston hay baling photos she wanted to showcase in her studio.

"Fifty."

Jillian huffed. "C'mon now. They're not *that* bad."

"How do you know?"

Unwilling to admit the relation, Jillian proceeded with negotiations. "Ten bucks."

Sasha filled a tray with four plates of food. "Now you're insulting me."

"Twenty. And I bet they'll tip you well." Stella might be a pain in the neck, but she wouldn't dare be seen as a woman who didn't leave a decent tip. Jillian had been out with her and Dad at a steakhouse in the city where the service had not only been terrible, it'd been nearly nonexistent. It'd taken over an hour to get their food, and when they did it was cold. Stella still left a twenty percent tip, claiming that maybe the waitress was having a really bad day. It was one quality she appreciated about the woman. "Please, Sasha."

"I don't know."

Jillian eyed the clock. If she could get Sasha to take this table, she could bring table twelve their check and slip right out the door. Stella and her dad would never even know she was here. "If they don't leave you twenty percent, I'll cover the difference."

"Twenty-five, then." She set the tray on her shoulder. "And when they stiff me my tip, you're paying that too."

Untying her apron and stuffing it in her little locker, her shoulders dropped in relief. She printed off the ticket for her last table and slipped back into the dining room to deliver it. "Hope everything was good for you folks." She couldn't remember the rancher's name, but she recognized his wife. They owned a sizeable acreage a dozen miles from town.

"It was excellent," the husband said.

"Say," said the wife, "I heard you're a photographer."

Jillian beamed a smile, but her fingers danced at her side. She could see Sasha standing at table six jotting down an order Stella was rattling off. But where was her dad? "I am."

"Heard you took some photos out at the Livingston Ranch."

"I did." She wasn't sure how that had already gotten around. She hadn't even had a chance to edit most of them.

"Do you have a website or something where I can check out your work?" The wife's eyes sparkled with excitement. "We might have a need of a photographer of our own. We're tearing down an old barn, and well, I want to document it."

"I do, actually." What a time to have a business card stuck in her apron, all the way back in her locker. Had her nerves not been on edge, it might've occurred to her to retrieve one. Instead, she speedily rattled off her web address. "I'm located on the Maxwell Ranch."

"Great! I'll be in touch."

Jillian spun away, her head turned over her shoulder in search of her still-missing dad, and bumped right into a customer. "I'm so sorry. I didn't see—"

"Jillian?"

"Dad." *Crap*. Crap, crap, crap. "Hey."

"What are you doing here?" He eyed the ticket in her hand, along with a ten and a twenty. "I thought you were working at your studio tonight." Her only saving grace was that the couple from table twelve had just walked out the door, obviously not expecting change.

Jillian's eyes darted to the kitchen, where she could see the blue trimmed outline of her escape. The back door was so close. "I'm picking up a to-go order." The yawn that followed that comment was genuine.

"I didn't realize they offered that option."

Mabel's Diner didn't offer to-go orders, though she was certain Mabel would make a killing if they did. She'd always been insistent that the interactions with customers throughout their dining experience was the key to keeping them coming back. "It's a new thing they're trying out. I'm one of the lucky guinea pigs."

"Ah, I see."

They stood there, the tension awkward and uncomfortable. "Well, I better grab my food and run."

"Why don't you join us?" her dad suggested. "Surely you're done editing photos by now?"

She wasn't, but only because she hadn't been home at all since the hike. "Thanks, Dad, but I have to get home. Early morning tomorrow." Which was also true since she had to fix Brantley breakfast. By this time, Sasha had returned to the kitchen and was shooting daggers at Jillian. Twenty-five was a steal.

Stella caught sight of her then and took up her dramatic waving, like one of those inflatable props flapping in the wind outside a car dealership. "Jill! Over here!"

"I can't stay, Dad."

"Come over for a minute, say hi?"

She always had a hard time saying no to her dad when he asked something of her with pleading eyes. The guilt she'd feel at turning him down would eat at her the rest of the night. "Only for a minute. After I take care of this," she said, lifting the ticket briefly.

"We didn't know you'd be here," Stella gushed, so much excitement in everything she said. As though finding her in a local restaurant of a town this small was such a crazy coincidence. She almost said something, but instead she smiled. "Jill, are you joining us?"

"It's Jillian, dear. She can't stay," her dad said. "She's waiting on some food."

Instead of sitting, Jillian leaned her hands on the back of a chair. If she sat, she'd be trapped and too tired to escape. And what would Sasha say when she came back with plates of food? No, she would have to take flight soon.

"Oh, that's too bad." Stella took a sip of what looked like their fresh-squeezed lemonade, but her wrinkled nose gave away her displeasure with the drink. "Are you and Brantley free tomorrow morning?" she asked. "We have a reservation for brunch at the hotel restaurant. Will you join us?"

If Jillian had kept her eyes on the table or out the window or anywhere else but on her dad, she might've been able to weasel her way out of this invitation. But she knew Brantley's schedule was pretty open. Holly had told her as much. *Freed him up this week so he's available to help you survive this wedding disaster.*

"It's a little brunch," her dad added. "Hotel makes a pretty good plate of banana pancakes."

Dang it, he remembered her weakness. It'd been weeks, maybe even months, since she had any. Her little apartment made things like pancake production difficult. Her last attempt resulted in a bruised elbow and a broken coffee mug.

"Won't be long at all. We have to run to the airport to pick up my nephew, Chad. The successful photographer. You remember him, don't you?"

This again. Jillian's cue to leave. "We'll meet you for brunch." Looking toward the kitchen, she pretended to nod at someone. Sasha caught her halfway and returned a scowl. If she didn't flee now, it might cost her double. "I think my food's ready. See you tomorrow."

She nearly tripped over her own feet on the way to the kitchen, avoiding Sasha's glare. Grabbing her coat, she darted out the back door and into the rain before she realized Brantley was supposed to pick her up.

She spun back around and tucked herself under a small awning to dig her phone out of her purse to call. But the string of text messages distracted her from that task. She scrolled through the updates about Milo being a good boy, and stopped on a single photo. One of Milo with a goofy grin, looking right at the camera.

"What a chump!"

Jillian: You have to let me in on your secret.
Brantley: Never ;)
Jillian: No way you got that picture without some serious bribery.
Brantley: You'll never know [insert evil laughter]

Despite the rain pouring around her and without an option to hide inside the diner before Brantley arrived, Jillian smiled. They'd been friends for so long, but never like this. Something was definitely different.

Brantley: You done?
Jillian: Yeah.
Brantley: On my way. Leaving Milo. He's
passed out.

Another snap showed her golden retriever sprawled on his back on Brantley's couch, all fours in the air.

Brantley: Sleeping like a baby.

She realized something in that moment. Something startling and frightening. "I can't be falling for him," she whispered to the rain. She'd get her heart broken; she was sure of it. "I can't."

CHAPTER 12

*B*rantley

"Does she know?" Edie asked Brantley.

They stood on the porch, watching Jillian stroke Buttercup, much to the horse's sheer pleasure. It amazed him how good she always was with the horses, despite being afraid to ride. He knew other riders who'd been bucked off and didn't care to go near a horse again. Jillian had never met Buttercup until today, and yet she greeted the mare as an old friend.

He shifted his weight to the other foot and slipped his hands into his front pockets. "She's great with Buttercup, don't you think?" He felt his great aunt's eyes boring into him. She wouldn't let it go so easily.

The screen door creaked as Edie pulled it open to slip inside—one more thing he needed to tend to soon. "Avoid my question if you want, but don't wait until it's too late." The door snapped shut before he could fully turn in her direction.

They came so he could replace a couple of shingles on the barn roof and exercise Buttercup. At the tail end of an uncomfortable brunch with Rodney and Stella, he insisted Jillian come along.

Jillian knew it was as per their agreement. He didn't say that in front of Rodney or Stella, but he mentioned the errand to give her a break before dealing with the wedding flower errand Stella had pawned off on them this afternoon.

"She's done this the whole time she's been here," Jillian complained after brunch once they were back in the safety of his Jeep. "She makes these innocent invitations, but they're never what they seem. She corners people into favors."

She'd been stressed, squeezing her fingers into her cheeks for most of the drive to Edie's. But once she saw Buttercup, her entire body relaxed. She really did love horses, and he hoped today might finally help her overcome her fear of riding.

They could have taken any of the horses at the ranch. She'd have believed his excuse, he knew. But he wanted Edie to meet her. For as long as they'd all lived in Starlight, it was odd really that Edie and Jillian had never met. Not intentionally anyway.

He watched his great aunt through her porch window as she shuffled around in the kitchen, no doubt readying a pot of coffee. Maybe he'd told Edie more than he should have about his feelings for Jillian.

He wanted a story like Edie and her husband Frank's, married fifty-two years before Frank passed away. He wanted someone to grow old with, and for him, it'd always been Jillian. But timing had never been on their side.

Jillian's laugh at Buttercup's insistent nuzzling at her ear carried to him through the warm summer breeze. His heart swelled at its intoxicating sound. What would he give to hear that sound for the rest of his life?

The thought rattled him to the core. Made him excited for what could come of this fake relationship if he played his cards right. Terrified of what he might lose if he didn't.

He hopped down from the porch and took some easy but deliberate steps toward Jillian. Her auburn hair, ever in its messy bun, glimmered in the sunlight like copper. She looked like a dream in those jeans and cowgirl boots he'd forgotten she had until the hay baling adventure. Now, she hardly took them off.

"Ready to take her for a ride?" he asked as he

approached. He tried to come off as indifferent, but the question made him nervous, too.

Jillian craned her neck back from the horse. "Maybe after some coffee?"

"Sure. Edie's got a pot on now." He lifted his arm, about to absently drop it around her shoulders. But she caught him mid-gesture and raised her eyebrows. "Kind of a habit this week." He turned away, shoving his hands into his jeans pockets. Maybe there would never be more between them.

"We don't have to pretend out here," she reminded.

Maybe he was foolish to think for once timing was on their side.

The screech of the screen door drew their attention. "Coffee's ready," Edie called. "Come have a cup."

The three sat around the table sipping their coffee, except today the comfortable silence he was so used to was interrupted by a gushing Jillian. "You have a lovely place, Mrs. West."

"Edie, please."

"It's so close to town, yet quiet and secluded in its own peaceful way."

"It's rather perfect, isn't it?" Edie smiled, but it didn't quite reach her eyes. He worried this morning had been a rough one for his great aunt. The bags under her eyes seemed to suggest sleep was fitful at best.

"I wish my studio had the views your property does."

He sipped on his coffee, adding an extra squirt of hazelnut creamer, as the two women chattered away about photography and horses and life. Conversation flowed so naturally, so easily between them. Despite the weariness tucked into Edie's eyes, her energy seemed to pick up little by little. He almost hated the idea of separating them.

"Why don't you two take Buttercup for a ride while I get started on lunch?" Edie suggested once all their cups were empty.

"Are you sure you don't need help?" Jillian's voice sounded innocent enough, but he wasn't fooled by her stalling tactics.

"Go ride, dear. Buttercup will enjoy your company immensely."

Unable to argue, Jillian allowed Brantley to lead her out onto the front porch. She hesitated at the steps, hand clinging to one of the posts, and he thought Jillian might be about to tell him. He'd never force her on a horse if she wasn't ready to ride. "Something wrong?"

"No."

Buttercup trotted along the fence to the barn with them, a pep in her step at the promise of a ride. She loved her trails. He wasn't sure how she'd feel about two riders since it had been years, but Edie seemed confident she'd do well.

He took his time saddling the horse. He wanted to give Jillian as much time as possible to get used to the idea. "You won't feel too crowded if we ride her together, right? Edie doesn't have any other horses."

"I don't mind." She slowly stroked Buttercup's neck.

When he could stall no more, he looked at Jillian. "Why don't you climb up first? I'll let you sit up front and take the reins." It was a risky suggestion. If she panicked, they might both be in trouble. But he hoped sitting behind her would help her feel secure.

Her fingers ran over the saddle horn in nervous strokes. Buttercup was about as docile as horses came, even with nervous riders. But the mare took a couple of uneasy steps at Jillian's hesitation.

"You need a hand?" he offered.

Without a reply, she slipped her foot into the stirrup, gripped the horn, and slung herself into the saddle. He waited to catch her if she didn't quite make the mount, but it wasn't necessary. "Here, take these." He handed over the reins.

The mare didn't seem to fuss with both him and Jillian for riders.

Having Jillian in front also gave him an excuse to put his arms around her, though for as slowly as they trotted, it wasn't necessary. Unlike before, though, Jillian didn't give him any funny looks when his arms went around her. "There's a trail I haven't taken in a while," he said against her ear, the scent of her lavender shampoo invading his senses. "It has a spot where I want to take that photograph."

"The sunrise photo?"

"Yeah." He felt a little guilty, keeping the truth from her. But he wasn't ready to talk about Paul. He wasn't the only one; Paul's best friend Mason had reenlisted to keep his distance. "I think it would be perfect. Maybe we go that Sunday after the wedding festivities are over?"

"I think we can work that in."

He wasn't ready to tell her the reason he knew the spot was great for a sunrise. It wasn't like he'd ridden out in the dark one morning to find it. No, he'd had a few too many after Paul's memorial service and stumbled his way down the trail on foot.

"I don't have my camera," Jillian admitted. "Stella had me so irritated about the flowers."

Jillian's camera was an extension of herself, something she never left home without. If she forgot it, the flower errand they'd been asked to take care of later was making her more uneasy than she let him know. "Don't worry about it today. Enjoy the scenery."

"It's a shame, too. Everywhere you turn out here, there are such perfect shots."

He pointed, purposely leaning his raised arm against Jillian's side, as the sunrise spot he found quite by accident appeared. "It's just up ahead."

He didn't want to admit it had been so long since he'd been up here. That after the morning he discovered it, he'd failed to return. Like he'd failed to return anywhere that reminded him too much of Paul.

The trail rounded along a rocky edge, the landscape dropping off several dozen feet below in a gradual rocky, weedy slope. The drop-off wasn't enough to kill someone, he had thought the morning he woke up with his face on the edge of the dirt trail, overlooking the ground below. But it was enough to bang someone up pretty good.

"Wow." Jillian turned to look at him over her shoulder, her lips closer to his than she should let them.

He wished he had a reason to kiss her. He'd been wishing that all week. What was the point of a fake relationship if he didn't get to kiss her even once?

"It's amazing, Brantley."

"You think it'll make a good picture?"

"You've got everything you need. The perfect frame." She held up her hands, making two Ls out of her fingers. "The mountains, the lake, the sky . . . It must be a breathtaking sunrise."

"It's the most amazing thing you've ever seen." That morning, he was certain Paul had been behind that sunrise. One grand gesture from beyond to let his brother know everything would be okay. It took months for him to reach that conclusion, and still he wasn't sure everything would ever be okay with Paul gone. But he was trying to believe it.

"Your mom is going to love it. I think it's a very sweet gift."

Guilt crept in again. Both at hiding the truth of the photo from Jillian and at the reminder he still hadn't called Mom as he promised Edie.

"I hope I do it justice." Someday he'd tell Jillian all the things about Paul she didn't know. He'd have to when she saw that photo framed and hanging on his living room wall.

"Here." Jillian tugged on his elbow, pulling him into the spot she'd been standing. "Lift your hands, like this." She made the L again and waited for him to do the same. "The key is to split the photo in thirds."

"Thirds?"

"Quiet, I'm teaching here." She wore that cute smile that usually left him speechless. "The rule of thirds. It helps with capturing a great visual. You want to split any frame into three sections, but both horizontally and vertically."

"I'm supposed to imagine nine little boxes?"

"I wish I had my camera. I have a grid mode that helps you get the hang of it. But for today, you'll have to pretend."

"Nine boxes."

She moved closer. "It's not the boxes that matter, but the points where your lines intersect." She tried to reach her arm over his to point at something within his imaginary frame, but his were lifted too high. "Stand still."

Slipping beneath his outstretched arms, she stood with her back to his chest. He tried to keep a small space between them for fear she might feel the insane beating of his heart. That lavender shampoo could be the death of him.

"Let's move your frame." Soft fingers tugged his wrists a little to the right and down. "There, now we have some good mountains, sky, and water."

"Should I zoom in?" Making jokes might be his only chance at hiding how much she affected him. At least she couldn't see his face.

"No zoom. Here are your lines." Jillian drew invisible lines with her finger. "See how the horizon's not in the middle?"

"We don't want that?"

"No." Jillian traced a line toward the top of his frame. "We have it along that top line to add some visual appeal with the mountains, and that lake. For the sunrise though, we might make the sky the upper two thirds since it'll be the star of the photo."

His arms burned a little at being outstretched for so long. "I don't know that I'll ever be your star student." He let his arms drop to his sides, but Jillian didn't leap away as he expected.

Instead, she turned to face him. "It takes time to

get the hang of it. But don't worry. I'll help you get the best sunrise photo possible."

The wind whipped a stray hair from behind her ear right across her nose. Her emerald eyes sparkled up at him, and he wondered if this might be one of those moments people talked about. One that changed everything.

As his hand lifted to brush away the strand of hair, Buttercup let out a loud, uneasy neigh. Her back legs moved from side to side, eyes wide at something in the trees.

"There's a fox." Jillian pointed into the tree line. The bushy orange tail was all he spotted.

"One bit her on the leg a few years back." He sighed, the moment gone. "We better walk beside her going back. She'll be a little nervous."

Jillian's relief seemed clearly visible. Her tense shoulders dropped, and her expression lightened. She'd been a brave trooper on the ride out, never once complaining. But she'd been stiff and quiet. It would take more than one ride to overcome her fears.

"Jilly—"

"I can walk her, if that's okay?"

 illian

Jillian felt a little shaky at Edie's kitchen table. She hadn't been in a saddle in three years. Though she couldn't have been on a calmer horse or safer than she'd been with Brantley riding behind her, she'd been afraid on their ride out. Afraid that Buttercup would get spooked and buck them both off down a rocky ledge.

"You have a nice ride?" Edie bustled from the counter, to the stove top, to the sink, and back again. Once more, she'd refused Jillian's help with lunch.

"Yes." She wrapped her fingers around the sweating glass of ice water as if it were a lifeline. It would take more than one ride to convince her she was safe riding again. Brantley had left the two women alone so he could replace a shingle on the barn before lunch was ready. She searched for some other topic. "You have such a lovely property."

"Why, thank you." Edie gazed out the kitchen window. "Frank and I waited almost a decade for this place to come up for sale. The second the rumor hit, we were standing on the front porch banging on the door." Edie turned and smiled, but Jillian could see the hint of pain in her soft gaze. What would it be like to love someone so much, to build a life together, and then be forced to live out years of it alone?

Stella's comment about Jillian not being the marrying type crept back in. Maybe she'd never know because she'd never find someone to grow old with. It might be a stretch if it'd only been Jason who broke her heart, but there were others. A string of failed relationships with the same result.

"Brantley seems to enjoy the time with Buttercup. Comes over about three times a week, you know."

"Does he?" It made sense. Edie was family, and she'd been without her husband more than two years, if she recalled right. "He's good with her."

"I think Buttercup's helped him a lot with Paul. But he still has a lot of healing left."

"He doesn't talk about his brother much."

"I suspect not." Edie folded a dish towel and tucked it over the oven handle. "Paul and I weren't as close as I am with Brantley. He wasn't really the ranching, ride-a-horse type. But I did get to enjoy his company a few times. He was a good man. An honorable man."

"Brantley still hasn't dealt with it, has he?"

Edie went to the front door and poked her head out, no doubt looking for Brantley. "They weren't that close growing up. I think Brantley's always regretted that, even before Paul passed away. That's why he joined the Army, you know."

She didn't know that, but it made sense. Paul had always planned to go into the Army, and everyone talked about their decorated war hero all the time he was away. But everyone in Starlight had been shocked at the news of Brantley enlisting. She'd never known him to express interest in joining the military.

The night before he was to get on a plane, she went to his cabin to ask why he was even going. The question had been burning inside her for the entire two weeks since he announced the news. He had done a pretty good job of avoiding her once the word was out. She hadn't understood it then, but she cared about him. More than she wanted to admit to herself, she realized now.

Then the rain started to pour, and she turned and left before he knew she came by.

"Paul was as shocked as anyone," Edie continued. "But he made the best of it. Pulled what strings he could to get his brother stationed on the same base so he could look after him." Edie checked one of her pots on the stove. "They had a trip planned for when Paul got back from his last deployment. Some national park tour or something. Brantley won't talk about it now."

"I guess I understand why." Paul only made it home from that deployment in a casket. "How did—"

"I hope you ladies left me something to eat," Brantley said through the screen door. He kicked off his boots on the front porch before letting himself inside. "I'm starving."

———

"I'm sorry she roped you into this, too," she apologized to Brantley for the fifth time in the ten blocks they'd driven.

"Jilly, it's fine."

"But it's *flowers*." Truth be told, she was glad he was coming with her. The last time she paid a visit to Peggy's Petal Paradise, she'd been picking out flowers for a wedding that never happened. She wasn't sure she could face going back to the boutique alone. Surely Peggy would have a dozen questions about the *almost* wedding and why it hadn't happened.

"Stella's already given us her selections,"

Brantley said. "I don't think we can mess anything up too badly." When she didn't respond, he added, "Fuchsia is a shade of yellow, right?"

"It's not yellow—" But he interrupted her with a hearty laugh.

"Jilly, relax." He parked the Jeep in front of the flower shop and pulled the key from the ignition, sitting a moment against the seat. "We're doing Stella and your dad a favor. We have more detailed instructions than a computer programmer could write."

She couldn't meet those dark eyes, so instead she stared at the curly purple font on the sign, decorated with a sprinkling of flowers. Seemed it had a fresh coat of paint since her last visit. "I know." She grabbed the door handle and pushed before she lost her nerve.

Her feet shuffled across the threshold, the light green of the walls capturing her attention first. The sign had gotten a fresh paint job, but the shop had not. Jillian's palms went cold, and she tucked her fingers into fists at her sides, her thumbs rubbing nervously. *I can't do this.*

Pivoting mere steps inside the store, she collided with Brantley. Her nose smashed into his chest, his addicting woodsy scent invading her senses.

"Jilly?"

Realizing he had no idea why she turned right into his arms, she took a step back and dipped her head to admire an arrangement in hopes she'd hide her reddened cheeks. "Too bad these are purple. They'd be perfect, don't you think?"

A warm hand brushed her forearm, fingers curling around it gently. "Talk to me."

"But those over there—"

"Jilly." This time, warning hung in his tone. The heat of his hand still on her arm caused her shivers.

She looked away from his fingers. *Stupid realizations.* "It's nothing."

"I don't believe—"

"Howdy!" Peggy herself greeted them as she emerged from an open door behind the front counter. "What can I do for the happy couple?"

She jumped back, Brantley's hand falling away. She hoped Peggy didn't remember her. She'd made a point to avoid this place since Jason demanded his ring back and boarded a plane for New York. She avoided anywhere that reminded her of that failed relationship.

"We need to select some flowers for a wedding," she replied.

"Oh!" Peggy clapped her hands together, her eyes enlarging behind her purple-rimmed glasses. Her entire body bounced with elation. "Congratulations! Young love is such a beautiful thing. When's your big day?"

"We're not—" Jillian started.

"Not us," Brantley jumped in. "We're helping

out her dad. He and his fiancée had an appointment with you today."

Peggy reached for a bursting planner littered with a rainbow array of sticky notes and opened it on the counter in front of her. "Are you sure?" Her eyes jumped immediately to Jillian's left hand.

Jillian shoved her hands in her back pockets. "We're sure."

"Well, maybe someday then." Peggy's smile lingered as she scanned her book, as if she hoped they'd confirm her wishes. But when neither said a thing, she asked, "What was the name?"

"Rodney Harper and Stella—"

"Ah, yes." Peggy ran her finger down her planner page. From this side of the counter, though upside down, Jillian could see that the page was completely filled with notes and doodles. "Stella called yesterday."

Of course she did. Jillian let out a soft sigh. No point in getting upset about it now. Stella and her ulterior motives . . . Jillian had made it inside the flower shop. Might as well see it through. "She gave us some instructions."

Peggy studied her a moment, as if trying to place her face. Jillian shuffled her feet, looking away. "I made some centerpiece mockups to show her. I have them in the back room." Peggy pointed over her shoulder. "Come with me."

From the narrow width of the storefront, Jillian

expected this room to be cramped. Instead, it felt open and light. Inviting even. A couple of cushy ivory loveseats sat against the far walls around a glass coffee table showcasing the arrangement samples. This wasn't something she remembered from her last visit. Had Peggy remodeled?

"Have a seat," Peggy directed. "But be careful. These couches like to swallow customers." She let out a little giggle at her own joke, while Jillian was still trying to relax.

"You sure you're okay?" Brantley asked against her ear.

She made the mistake of meeting his eyes and almost caved. She wanted to tell him how hard this was for her. How it twisted her heart into tangled vines to be so blatantly reminded of such a failure. How Stella's comment about her not being the marrying type seemed to gut her, even though she knew better than to let it.

"Let's get this over with."

———

"She did *not* ask you to do that!" Jillian's mom all but shouted on the other end of the phone. Today, she would give anything for her mom to be sitting across the little table in her studio. Mom knew the truth about her life, had even been there on opening day to celebrate with her, and eventually she was the shoulder to cry on when Jason fled.

"Stella doesn't *ask*."

"You sure you don't want me to fly up there? I haven't used any of my sick days this year. I could come down with a stomach bug."

"Don't do that, Mom." She didn't want her mom emptying her savings on a plane ticket and hotel room. Her dinky apartment wasn't exactly accommodating for guests. As it was, she slept on a sofa bed that Milo mostly hogged.

"I can't believe how insensitive it all is. Didn't your father say *anything*?"

"He doesn't know."

"What?"

She buried her face in her hands and let it drop onto the table. Milo, concerned, shoved his nose up under her arms until she looked at him. "I never told him Jason and I were engaged, much less that we broke up."

"I don't understand."

"Yeah, join the club." She moaned dramatically, then spilled the entire fabricated story as Dad knew it. The overexaggerated success of her business, the close call at the diner, the fake relationship with Brantley.

"I never understood why you didn't just date that boy for real. What's with all this pretend stuff?"

"Mom!"

"What? I'm just saying . . . He's an attractive young man. Polite and hardworking, if I recall. Always been crazy about you."

She laughed at that. "Yeah, right. Now you're making stuff up. Mom, I have to go. I have some photos to edit, and for once, that's not a lie."

"You know, Jilly Bean, telling the truth is so much easier than keeping all your lies straight. Remember that."

"Love you, Mom." She clicked the end call button before any more unsolicited advice could come through the phone. Yes, of course her mom was right. But she'd gone this long with the charade, it was much easier to finish it out. Her dad and Stella would leave after the wedding and probably never visit again.

As for the comment about Brantley being crazy about her . . . she wanted to believe it was true, but she couldn't allow that fantasy to take root. She refused to let her silly, inconvenient feelings jeopardize what they had as friends. If her mom was wrong about Brantley's feelings and she ventured to act on her own, she might ruin that friendship. It wasn't worth the risk.

CHAPTER 14

*B*rantley

Brantley carried a tripod up the steps to Jillian's childhood home, following behind her to the front door. She'd tried getting out of the shoot again this morning, he discovered, but the realtor couldn't find another last-minute photographer and seemed irritated at Jillian for stalling.

"Jilly, you need to shoot this house today," he told her at breakfast. He didn't need to mention that refusing to do so might sever what was currently her main source of income. Without her real estate jobs, she might not be able to keep her business afloat. "You want them to keep sending you listings to shoot, right?"

She glared, but it was that cute glare that meant he was right. "Someday I won't have to do these at all."

He waited two steps below as she fished a key out of her pocket and unlocked the door to the screened-in porch. "We used to sit out here a lot. On a swing." Her voice held steady, and he hoped she'd taken the time she needed to prepare herself. "My mom and me."

"How is your mom?" He closed the front door behind them and awaited instructions with the tripod. He still needed to call his own. He quieted the nagging voice in his head that reminded him.

"Desperate to come to my rescue, but doesn't want to be within a thousand miles of my dad. She won't say that out loud."

The vacant house, bare of window coverings, invited in a lot of natural light. A spacious L-shaped room began right inside the front door. A brick fireplace sat directly across from that. He could see Jillian curled up on a couch watching a TV above the mantel. So many things he wanted to ask but didn't dare.

"I usually start with the kitchen," she explained. "Can you bring the tripod?"

The kitchen and dining area were to the rear of the house, separated from the living room by a half wall and a transition from ivory carpet to dark gray tile. He set the tripod on the breakfast bar.

"Doesn't even look the same." Jillian fidgeted with her camera settings and aimed at the wall, probably catching his arm in the frame. "They've redone almost everything. The floors, the wall colors. Even the cabinets—repainted."

The emotion he saw in her eyes the day they drove by was missing now. He didn't know if she'd simply been caught off guard the other day or if she'd managed to shove down her feelings instead of dealing with them. He couldn't blame her if it was the latter. He'd done a good bit of that himself when it came to his brother.

"I was so mad at my mom when she sold this house," Jillian said. "But I didn't understand things back then."

He backed out of the kitchen and lingered in the living area on the other side of the half wall so she could get the best angles of the kitchen. He watched in awe as she moved the tripod to different areas, fiddled with the lights, the camera settings. Jillian Harper was a natural behind the lens.

He wanted to tell her so. Almost did.

"My mom didn't want to stay after Dad left. She'd spent enough years moving around the country with him. But she stayed for me. Because she knew this was the first place that truly felt like home for me." Jillian shifted the tripod. "Get that light?"

He flipped a nearby wall switch. "My mom left days after Paul's service." Guilt crept in at the promise he made Edie to call her. He'd been putting it off, finding any excuse he could. But he'd shoved Jillian out the door to shoot the house instead.

"You and your brother, were you close?" Jillian peered through the viewfinder on her camera despite the digital display screen on the back. Something he'd seen her do with every shot.

"Five years apart."

Jillian looked at him from over her shoulder. "That's not what I meant." The green of her eyes was more prominent in the natural light. He turned away, afraid she might be able to see into his soul. There were emotions and fears lingering in the depths of him he didn't want Jillian to discover.

"We didn't have much in common growing up."

"But you both served in the Army?"

"Yes." His chest tightened, as if someone was squeezing it. He slowed his breathing with deep, discreet breaths, a trick he taught himself after too many people worried after his welfare. He didn't want their attention or pity. Paul was the one who made the ultimate sacrifice, not him.

"In Alaska, right?" Jillian carried the tripod to the room's edge where tile met carpet, aiming the camera into the living room. His cue to move.

"Yeah. Fort Wainwright."

"Kind of cool, huh? You and Paul and Mason ending up in the same unit."

He always suspected Paul had something to do

with that. It wasn't common for brothers to end up in the same unit, especially if they joined a couple of years apart. But Paul knew people, and everyone loved him. "Yeah, it was a perk."

"I never understood why you did it," she continued. "Why you joined up. I thought you lived and breathed the ranching life. Everyone did."

He'd let her press plenty. He had talked about this with her more today than he had with anyone since the memorial service. Even Edie couldn't break through the barrier he put up. "Never understood why you were engaged to that New Yorker."

She disappeared around a corner into a main floor bedroom. "I was stupid." She spoke so matter of factly, and much to his relief, allowed the subject change without question. "Jason was never going to stay in Starlight. But I was dumb enough to believe him when he said he wanted to."

"He was a jerk." He had known her ex only slightly. He'd kept his distance from Jillian when they were together. But it hadn't stopped him from fixing up the cabin Holly wanted to rent out to her. And he hadn't been able to stay away on opening day. He'd witnessed the breakup from a distance. "He didn't deserve you."

"The funniest part of it all, now that I can laugh about it, was that he asked me to give the ring back. I mean, who does that?" She folded the tripod legs and eyed the staircase off the front door. He wondered if she had ever slid down the polished oak banister as a kid. He bet she had. "If you're going to leave a girl you asked to marry you high and dry, at least let her pawn the ring so she can spend it on something frivolous and impractical."

He laughed at that, enjoying the twinkle in her eyes at her joke. The sound of her laughter always made him so light, so happy. "What would you've done with the cash?"

"Equipment for my studio. Better lighting, backdrops, lens. That sort of thing." He followed to the top of the stairs and watched as she set up the tripod in the hallway, pointed into a bedroom. "I know, not exactly reckless or exciting."

"Maybe not, but—"

Incessant knocking sounded from the front door, followed by a few rings of the doorbell. They looked at each other, eyebrows drawn in. Didn't seem Jillian was expecting company.

"That's odd," she said. "She told me there weren't any showings today."

"Realtor? Nosy neighbor?" he suggested.

Leaving her camera in one of the bedrooms, Jillian walked down the stairs and to the front door with him as another burst of knocking echoed. "Seriously, it's an empty house." Though her tone flared with annoyance, her fingers wrapped around his arm.

He opened the door, prepared for anything

except the two people standing across the threshold. "Mr. Harper?"

"Stella?" Jillian chimed in.

"Brantley, we saw that Jeep of yours outside. Wondered what on earth you might be doing here. Rodney told me all about this place, and it looked empty." Stella craned her neck to look around them, still doing their best to block the doorway. "Why are you two here?"

Jillian's grip on his arm tightened. Telling the truth would blow Jillian's cover story, and a good bit of her dignity.

"We, uh . . ."

"I saw this house came up for sale." He jumped in when Jillian struggled to form a single coherent sentence. He couldn't let that go down in this house of all places, with Jillian's future stepmother standing at the front door. "Thought it might be time to look for something a little more permanent than my rancher's cabin." It wasn't true, of course. He'd built that cabin with the intention of living out the rest of his days there.

"Where's your realtor?" Stella repeated, her efforts to see inside relentless. She moved a couple of steps forward, her arm now wedged against the door frame. Inch by inch, she seemed determined to get across that threshold.

"Sweet Pea, are you two talking about buying a house together?" Rodney asked. "*This* house?"

Brantley looked at Jillian then, his eyes pleading for her to go along with it.

"It was a surprise," Jillian said finally. Though the slight quiver in her voice worried him. Was she okay with her dad standing on the front porch of *this* house? Then there was Stella . . .

"I didn't realize you two were that serious," Stella said. "It being two years and all and no ring. But a house . . ." For once, Stella didn't have much to say. "I guess it makes sense why you've been ignoring my texts."

Rodney aimed his stern gaze at Brantley. "That's a big commitment."

"Yes, sir." This was going south, he feared. But what else could he do? If they knew the real reason Jillian was here, Stella would no doubt belittle what success she had achieved with her own business. "We haven't decided anything official."

"Can we come in?" Stella pushed. "I'd love to see the place. Rodney's told me so much about it."

Jillian's fingers shackled his arm so tightly he was certain there'd be marks left behind. This was about more than being caught with a camera, he realized. It was principle. "We can't let anyone else in until our realtor gets back."

"We'll wait," Stella fired back.

"Actually, we're a little busy at the moment."

"But—"

"Life decisions on the line and all." His words

seemed to sink in with Rodney, but they didn't have the desired effect on Stella.

"Stella, this isn't the best time," Rodney said, tugging on her arm. But Stella wasn't budging. It appeared she didn't understand the irony of the house or the reason it was impolite to insist she see inside the home Jillian had grown up in with both of her parents.

"We'd like some time to ourselves, if you two don't mind?"

"Just a peek?"

Out of ideas, he turned to Jillian and swept her into his arms. He cupped her cheek and drew her in for a kiss so suddenly she barely had time to register what was happening. Her lips were stiff against his own. Had he made the wrong move?

"Surely you two can do that another time," Stella said.

Then Jillian fell into the kiss. Maybe to make it convincing for Stella, because she knew as well as he did that it would take more than a single flat kiss to make them go away. Maybe, just maybe, a small part of her wanted to see what it was like. He could hope anyway.

It took only seconds for the pretending to blend into something real. He'd waited years to kiss Jillian. He'd dreamt about this moment for so long he didn't hold back a thing.

"Hun, let's go," he vaguely heard Rodney say.

As the kiss deepened, Jillian's hand combed through the hair at the back of his neck. He heard the screen door slam shut. Brantley wished time would stop so he could kiss Jillian forever. All the sleepless nights he'd spent in the Army wishing he could hear her voice, all the missed opportunities, all those boyfriends he watched her date only to have her heart broken, faded away.

Jillian was the first to pull back. "They're gone." She stumbled a few steps away, adjusting her messy bun. "Thinking on your feet there?" Her words came out breathlessly, her cheeks flushed.

"I didn't know what else would work." He fought to catch his own breath. "Didn't even know if that would."

"But telling them we were moving in together was the ticket?"

He tried not to let his heart drop into the bottom of his chest. He was certain she felt the passion of that kiss, too. It was much too potent, too powerful to leave her unaffected. "I didn't think you wanted Stella in this house."

"You're right, it makes me a little crazy that she'd even come here." Jillian marched up the stairs. "They're gone now." She ambled on toward the rooms left to shoot—as if no kiss had ever happened, much less the best kiss of her life.

He'd hoped it was. Because it'd certainly been the best of his.

$\mathcal{J}$*illian*

Jillian had been ignoring Stella's texts and calls since the flowers had already been selected. It was almost too much, all these little favors turning into more *and* dragging her friends along for the ride. She'd spent the evening before at her computer desk with her phone turned off.

"We ready to go?" Holly asked as she slipped inside her studio later that afternoon.

"Almost."

It'd been wonderful to lose herself editing photos last night. She started by going through the entire collection she took at the Livingston Ranch, picking which ones to move to her special editing folder. *The first cut*, she always called them. She even sent Violet a couple to preview via email.

She nearly broke her phone silence to text Brantley, though. It'd been his idea for her to bring her camera out there, after all, and he'd been on to something, whether he knew it or not. She suspected he did. Why had she been so resistant to stretching outside her comfort zone? Sure, she always imagined she'd be constantly booked for special events like weddings and milestone birthdays. But it was eye opening how much of the ranching life was special to the people of this town.

She'd continued editing late into the night with the knowledge she might be making instant oatmeal for Brantley's breakfast the next morning.

"We could skip this dress fitting, right?" she pleaded to her best friend. She was done with the listing photos from earlier today and had already sent those off to the realtor. But now she wanted to keep working on the other photos, the ones she hoped to showcase on her walls and her website. "We already did the important one."

"You might not have as much to fear, but I want to make sure there's not enough room to store a couple of bowling balls in my dress top, thank you, busty Cousin Betty." Holly tugged her right out of her chair, away from her computer. But not before she caught the image on the screen. "Does Brantley know you took that?"

Jillian shook her head. "No. I was going to surprise him."

"It's a great photo. But I think I have some bad news for you."

"Yeah? What?"

"Milo might like him better than you." Holly laughed at her own joke, but it was enough to get Jillian out the door. "Where is that dog of yours anyway?"

"Brantley took him for the afternoon," she admitted, suddenly wishing she'd kept Milo at home. Holly was certain to make something more of all this than there was. She wasn't ready to tell her about the staged kiss that maybe hadn't felt quite so fake. "He knew we had the dress fitting. Said he could take Milo with him to check a broken fence. That dog loves riding in the ATV."

"You two have sure been spending a lot of time together."

Jillian opened the passenger door of Holly's truck and climbed inside before she was forced to respond on the spot. Holly had agreed to drive on the off chance they ran into Stella. She was less likely to recognize them in the truck than Jillian's car.

"You freed up his schedule to help me out."

"Maybe." Holly sped down the driveway, leaving

a dust cloud behind them. "But maybe this fake relationship isn't so *fake* after all."

"Don't be ridiculous." But her comeback didn't leave her heartbeat any calmer. Not after that kiss. She'd tried to play it off as though it meant nothing, that it hadn't completely spun her world in crazy fast circles. It was a tactic to get rid of her dad and Stella, that was all. "Of course it is."

"We've been friends since the first day you moved to Starlight." Holly pulled a pair of sunglasses from a center dashboard compartment and slipped them on. "You've never been able to lie to me. I always know when you're hiding something."

She couldn't argue. No one knew her better than her best friend. She should be able to confide in Holly about her confusing feelings for Brantley. She wanted to confide in someone. But something kept her tongue-tied. To voice those emotions and fears would make them much too real.

"I heard you finally shot that house you grew up in," Holly said. Her peace offering, for now, it seemed. But she wasn't fooled. The topic of Brantley would come up again.

"I need the money."

"What have you been doing this week to grow your business?"

"Twice in one week, huh?" Jillian asked, relieved to be switching topics. "I've been working on those photos from the hay baling operation at the

163

Livingston Ranch. Holl, I really thought it was a waste of time. But I've been going through those photos since last night, and I can't believe what I'm finding. Special events . . . they're so much more than I ever gave them credit for."

"You're excited. This is good!"

"I've been so stuck on only shooting weddings and special occasion parties that this new path never occurred to me." She almost said it was Brantley's idea, that he pushed her to bring her camera. But they'd finally gotten off the topic of him, and she wasn't ready to start up again. "And I already have another potential client for something similar."

"That's great!" Holly pulled in front of the seamstress's tiny shop a block and a half from the diner. Jillian couldn't wait for the day she no longer needed those extra shifts. But if it weren't for those tips, there were months she might not have been able to pay her electric bill.

Inside a small dressing room, Jillian shimmied into the gaudiest bridesmaid dress she'd ever lain eyes on. The hot pink mermaid contraption came with way too many ruffles on the short sleeves and bottom half of the dress. But it was the bedazzled heart placed above one hip that really took the cake.

"I still can't believe we have to wear these," she said apologetically.

"Don't forget the matching hair accessory." Holly laughed, plopping a hot pink bow on top of Jillian's head as they both faced the mirror. It clashed comically with her auburn hair.

"This is mortifying."

"It's not your day," Holly reminded. "It's only for a few hours. Then you can change into something that won't scare off wildlife and small children."

"But there'll be pictures."

"And we'll laugh about them for years to come. I'm in one of these dresses too, you know. Might as well own it."

The seamstress knocked on the door, stepping inside. Jillian's dress fit fine but for its hem, while Holly's still needed minor adjustments in the bust area. With promises to have the final adjustments done that same day, Jillian and Holly prepared to change.

"Don't you two look like a dream!" Stella boomed as she paraded into the changing room. "Those dresses are absolutely stunning, aren't they?"

"They're something," Jillian said with a forced smile. She hoped by avoiding the hotel for the final fitting they'd avoid Stella too. She should've known better. Stella's mere unexpected presence already had her tense, waiting for the angle.

"Best part is they're so versatile you can wear them again, don't you think?"

"You here for a dress fitting, too?" Holly asked,

saving them both from having to answer that trap of a question.

"Oh, no, my dress is all ready to go. You should see it! It's truly a work of art."

Jillian braced for whatever was coming. She'd grown so used to Stella's traps these past few days that it seemed pointless to escape now until she at least knew what she was in store for. "Were you out doing some shopping?"

"I was hoping you had a little time tonight," Stella said, a twinkle in her eye that bordered on crazy.

It felt like a trap. A big, bad trap.

"Actually, she's doing a job for me," Holly jumped in.

"Surely you can reschedule that?" Stella asked in that sickening sweet tone. "It's not every day that a charming photographer graces the presence of Starlight, after all, or offers up his time to take someone under his wing."

Chad.

"I'm sorry to put a damper in your plans, but I had to book Jillian a month ago so she could fit me in. I'm not willing to cancel my appointment." Holly's shoulders squared, her tone gentle but fierce. She reminded Jillian of a mama bear prepared to attack should a threat present itself.

"Maybe Chad can help?" Stella offered. "He takes the most amazing photographs! I sent you a link to the gallery on his website. You could learn so much from him."

Jillian had never actually believed blood could boil, but for as hot as her skin felt, she wondered if it were truly possible. How could Stella keep dismissing the fact that Jillian owned a photography business? Though she wasn't one to presume she had learned it all, she was good. Really good. She'd won ribbons at state fairs, artistic and professional awards. A couple of magazines had even featured her work. "I can't tonight. I have a client."

"Oh, well, that's too bad." Stella, still blocking their only exit, dug in her purse. "Here." She shoved a business card at Jillian. "He was generous enough to provide his cell. You should call him."

The wedding was only two days away. Two more days and she could put all this nonsense behind her and get back to what mattered; growing her business. She took the card, only because she didn't think Stella would let them leave if she refused. "We have to get changed and be on our way. I still need to grab my equipment."

"You'll be at the rehearsal dinner tomorrow?" Stella asked as they ushered her out the door and tried to close it.

"Yes, we'll be there," Holly answered, pushing the door the final two inches until it clicked shut. She deadbolted it too. "I'm not taking any chances."

They had to help each other out of their dresses

as the silky material tended to plaster itself on its victims in certain areas.

"All this time I was worried that Stella and my dad would stumble on to my studio and see what a failure I am," said Jillian. "But have you ever once heard that woman ask *where* my studio is? It's like she can't even acknowledge I have one."

"Maybe you should head to the lake," Holly suggested. "You need some paddleboarding time pronto."

———

Jillian felt like a coward, hiding out in Brantley's cabin to avoid her future stepmonster.

The sun had been shining when she left for the dress fitting. Perfect weather for a paddle boarding escape. But she'd no more than opened the shed to retrieve her board when the sky opened up and rained poured relentlessly. Instead, she had fled to the safety of Brantley's cabin.

But only because he had Milo.

She'd about had her fill of Stella's passive-aggressive comments for one day. The nerve of her to suggest *Chad* of all people mentor her! He'd only started his career in photography a year ago. Jillian had been studying it since high school.

Brantley was a little surprised to see her, drenched on his front porch. But he invited her in, offered her a dry T-shirt and a fleece blanket to curl up with on his couch while he made a pot of coffee.

"You sure are full of surprises," she told him. Milo had passed out on the couch, head in her lap. He let out the occasional sleep-bark-growl. He wasn't happy about the rain either, but at least he could nap without a care.

Brantley poured grounds into his well-used but quite fancy coffee maker. "What do you mean?"

He was gracious enough not to ask what the latest Stella disaster entailed. Lucky. Because she didn't feel like talking about it.

"I didn't really get a chance to look around last time I was here. The whole panicked thing and all. This . . ." Jillian moved her hand around the room. "It's so—"

"Nice?" Brantley offered with his quirky smile. One she was growing a little too fond of lately.

"I was going to say unlike you."

Brantley closed the lid to the coffee maker, pushed a button, and pulled coffee mugs from the cupboard. "I don't think you know me as well as you think you do. We're not teenagers anymore, Jilly."

Something about the way he said that nickname gave her shivers. She looked away from his unexpectedly smoldering gaze and busied herself with stroking Milo's neck. Memories from last night invaded her mind. The caress of his fingers down her arm. The feel of his stubble beneath her fingertips.

Then there was the pesky fact that his T-shirt smelled of his woodsy cologne.

"Tell me more about your brother." It was a risky topic, considering how it went the last time she asked. But it was sure to break whatever was happening between them.

"What do you want to know?" The question, asked so easily, was no doubt packed full of reservation if the thin line around his closed lips was any indication.

She knew some things about Paul West. But unlike Brantley, Paul never spent much time on the family ranch. With the five-year age difference between him and his brother, she never got to know Paul as well as she did Brantley. Of course, here in this cabin, surrounded by things that made it look like a home, she wondered if he was right. Did she really know Brantley West at all? "Well, you said you two weren't close."

"Not growing up, no." Mugs shuffled along the countertop. "We didn't have much in common. I was always out here, and Paul was always tinkering with something or another. Computer. Camera. Electronics geek."

That sounded about right, from what she already knew. But she wanted more. She fought the urge to ask again, stroking Milo instead. The dog kicked a couple of times in his sleep, no doubt after some dream rabbit.

"It's what got him the intelligence spot in the Army. Made him a good leader, too." Brantley opened the fridge and pulled out a container of creamer. Hazelnut if Jillian read the container right. But she was glued to the couch, too afraid of what she'd do if she got up. She'd want to touch him. To comfort him. And here in his cabin, there was no one to act for. Nothing to excuse her actions if things took a wrong turn.

"You two got closer in the Army, then?" She didn't think he was going to say too much more without prompting.

"Yeah, something like that."

Milo startled awake at a boom of thunder. He searched the cabin, a frantic look in his eyes as he oriented himself. Within a few seconds, he calmed and let his eyes fall shut again. "Why did you get out?" Jillian asked. "Of the Army? Mason signed back up, but . . ." She didn't quite know how to ask what she wanted, so she let her words trail off instead.

"Family." But the word was followed with a disbelieving laugh. "Of course, I didn't expect my mom to pick up and move the day after the memorial service."

On the couch, she didn't know what to say to that, so she sat still. The aroma of freshly brewed coffee carried to her now, but she'd no more interrupt what was happening than send Milo out in the rain.

Brantley had never opened up to her this much before, and once their little fake relationship deal was over, she wasn't sure he would again.

Brantley carried a cup of coffee over and sat beside her on the couch. Milo's eyes opened, his tail thunking on the other side as Brantley scratched him behind the ear. "The problem was, Paul and I were never that close. I wanted to be. I thought joining the Army would do that. That maybe he'd be proud of me, and we'd suddenly become the kind of brothers who spent a lot of time together. Did things together."

She placed her hand on top of his before she could think better of it. Brantley pulled her fingers in tighter, but his gaze never left the rain streaking down his living room window.

"I wanted to be closer to Paul, but I never tried. Not really."

"Brantley—"

"Now it's too late." He took a deep breath, as though he might be contemplating how much to say. But with parted lips, he leaned back against the couch and took a sip of coffee.

"When was the last time you went to see him?" she asked, hoping her question was careful enough.

"It's been a year."

Jillian could put the pieces together on her own. He hadn't been to the cemetery since the service. "You think it might be time to go?"

"Maybe."

So many words fought their way to the surface, but she didn't let any of them out. The edge in his tone meant he was done talking about this today. She loosened her fingers from his, gently lifted Milo's head, and slipped out from beneath him on the couch. The dog immediately curled into a ball, wrapping his tail around the outside of his body. "Bathroom?" Jillian asked.

Brantley pointed down the only hall.

At the sink, she ran some water and dabbed a little on her temples. She came here to escape the madness of the wedding festivities, but she'd found a whole other problem.

"No," she said to herself in the mirror. Her disheveled hair was frizzy from the rain, strands hanging around her cheeks. She used to wear it down almost all the time. But since she gave that ring back, it hadn't seemed to matter.

"No," she repeated. "You're not falling for him, Jilly." That kiss had haunted her all day. She wanted to go to him now, cup his jaw in her hands, and kiss away the pain. She wanted to spend the evening curled up with him on the couch while the storm raged outside. These new feelings scared her.

None of it was worth jeopardizing their friendship. She couldn't imagine her life without Brantley in it. She'd grown rather fond of calling him when something in the cabin needed repairing, of their morning breakfasts, of his company in general. If she made the wrong move, she could spoil everything.

After more than a few reasonable minutes, she stilled her nerves and prepared to rejoin him in the living room. The pitter patter of heavy rain drops on the metal roof warned her the storm had no plans of letting up. She'd have to tough it out. Nothing worse than a wet dog trapped in a confined space. She didn't feel like cleaning up the studio if Milo tracked mud everywhere.

In the hallway, she froze. Her eyes caught the open crack of a door, and through it she saw color. Lots of color.

Curiosity drew her closer, while caution forced her to crane her neck out into the living room to ensure Brantley hadn't moved from the couch.

The door was open several inches, and as she tiptoed closer, it became quite clear that the blurs of color were photographs. Landscapes. Some framed and hanging on the walls. Others stacked against a desk and the walls. Almost all of them included the sun.

"Sunrises."

Her heart pattered in her chest, confusion swimming through her mind. Brantley had asked her to teach him to take pictures. How to shoot the sunrise. But it seemed apparent he already knew. Even the Nikon camera on the desk was of high quality. Something only someone who knew what they were doing would dare to spend the money on.

Why did he lie to me?

Her heart hammered in her chest. She couldn't fathom a reason he would choose to humiliate her, but no normal person asked for photography lessons when they were practically a pro themselves.

Whatever his angle, she wasn't having it. Rain or no rain, she had to go. She had to go now.

She backed out of the room and spun. Right into Brantley's chest.

"What are you doing back here?" he asked, any familiar lightness she usually found in his tone gone.

She met his eyes for only a moment, but it was enough to see the flare of anger there. "You *lied* to me." She pushed passed him in the tight hallway and clipped on Milo's leash. "You wanted to make a fool out of me." She sprinted out the door and into the rain.

CHAPTER 16

*B*rantley

Brantley ran a frustrated hand through his hair. He still gripped the door knob to the room with Paul's photos. He needed to install a lock. Jillian had been gone from his couch for a few minutes, but he didn't presume she'd gone snooping and opened doors on her own. No, the dang thing probably opened on its own again and gave her quite the display.

Jillian didn't know much about Paul. Probably had no idea at all that he was into landscape photography. Most people didn't. To Starlight, he was the hometown military hero. Though her misunderstood reaction was extreme and unexpected, he couldn't blame her for being upset.

Pulling the door closed and tugging a couple of extra times to ensure the latch caught, he went back to the living room to find his phone. He could understand her urge for flight, but in the storm it seemed reckless.

He tried to call her first, but she didn't answer. He waited the few minutes he expected it took for her to drive that little car across the ranch, back to her cabin. The cloth seats would be covered in muddy paws.

Brantley: I can explain, Jilly.

He waited several minutes for the three trailing dots graphic to pop up showing a response in progress. Nothing.

Brantley: Those aren't mine.

He almost typed out another text, telling her they were Paul's. But he wasn't yet ready to go down that road. No, if he did, she'd want to know much more than he was ready to disclose. The best thing, he decided, was to let her cool off tonight. He'd drive by a little later to make sure she made it home safely.

Pouring himself another cup of coffee, he watched the rain streak down his front window. A flash of lightning lit up the sky.

His phone sat on the black granite counter in front of him, one of Paul's sunrise shots set as the lock screen. Guilt crept in again. It'd been a year since he talked to his mom. A year since he answered any of her calls. A year since he even tried to reach out. They might've held differing opinions on a lot of things, but they were both hurting over the loss of Paul.

He found her number and pushed call before he could talk himself out of it. It rang four times, and he was about to hang up when someone answered. "Hello?"

"Mom?"

An uncomfortable pause lingered, and he feared she'd hang up on him. They'd exchanged less than kind words when she left Starlight. "Brantley," she finally said. The word came out tired, maybe slightly irritated. As though she wasn't ready to do this today.

"Is it a bad time?" He already wished he could end the call. Something like static or wind came through the phone. "Are you at work?"

"I retired. Four months ago."

Had he heard that, maybe from Holly? She was the best at keeping in touch with their extended family. Surely she mentioned it, but he had probably tuned it out. "How's that been?"

"I'm sitting on a beach in the Cayman Islands, so not terrible." Was there a hint of sarcasm in her voice? Sarcasm was his mother's main charm. But he couldn't see whether that mischievous twinkle danced in her eyes.

His tongue tied into knots, unsure what to say.

"Everything okay, Brantley?"

"Yeah." He sipped on his coffee again. "I wanted to see how you were doing." So much more to say. Apologies to extend. But he couldn't find the right words. Not today.

"I'm doing okay."

"Good. I'm glad to hear it." He emptied his cup and carried it to the sink. Any more coffee, and he might not sleep tonight. "Very glad to hear it."

"I've got to meet a friend for dinner," she said. After an uncomfortable pause, she added, "You should think about visiting. I moved to Phoenix, you know. I'll be home next week."

"I don't know—"

"Think about it. That's all I ask."

He couldn't bear to tell his mom no. Not after their first conversation—even if a little awkward and painful—in over a year. He could think about taking that trip. Didn't mean he had to do it. "Okay."

———

"What do you mean they're not yours? Of course they're yours!"

Brantley had hoped with a night to sleep on it, Jillian might come to the conclusion that another explanation existed. But if the cold Pop-Tarts on his plate the following morning were any indication, she hadn't budged an inch. Even Milo, lying at his feet looking up with sad eyes, seemed disappointed they weren't eating something better. Brantley reached down to pat his head in apology.

"If you come with me, I'll explain it all."

Jillian refused to look up from her computer monitor. She'd been clicking away on something since he arrived. "No."

Instead of the cup of coffee she'd been leaving for him, she set a bottle of water in its place. At least he had two cups at home before coming over. He twisted off the cap, letting out a sigh. "You need me to come to that rehearsal dinner tonight, right?"

"Yeah." It took a moment, but the reality of what he was implying seemed to settle in. She rolled back her chair and turned to face him. "You wouldn't."

"I would." He lied, of course. He wouldn't force Jillian to go alone to that dinner. Stella would notice his absence and drill her until she caved. Maybe it made him pathetic, but he'd never leave Jillian in a bind.

"You're not really taking that sunrise photo for your mom, are you?"

A sigh escaped. "No."

She pushed out her chair. "Aha! I knew it." Dang it, even her narrowed eyes pointed at him like fiery daggers were cute.

He focused on his Pop-Tart, breaking off a corner and tossing it to Milo. At least the dog was still on his side, even if a bit disappointed at the meager ration.

"Why, Brantley? Why would you want to humiliate me?" She was pacing again, and it was all he could do to remain in his seat. "I can't even figure out *why* you'd ask me to help you do something you're already very good at. It doesn't make sense."

Slowly he finished his last bite of cold blueberry Pop-Tart and carried his paper plate to the round wastebasket near her desk. "You about done?"

Her jaw dropped open. But she finally quit ranting.

"I can't take photos. That was always Paul." He reached for his hat and set it on top of his head. No matter how much he told himself he could handle this conversation, it still felt like lead sat in the bottom of his stomach. "You coming or not?"

Back at his cabin, Brantley's hand rested on the door knob. He tried to discreetly take a deep breath. As it was, the cold, hard knob was the only thing hiding the trembling. He'd never shown another person this room. He told himself it was because Paul's work wasn't his to show. But the truth was darker than that.

"Brantley?" Those pursed lips were keeping in a lot more words. He felt a little guilty for his tactic to get her over here, threatening to bail on the rehearsal dinner. But Jillian deserved to know the truth.

"Paul was the photographer," he finally said as the knob turned slowly in his grip. "I don't know how to do much more than snap a button on a camera. But Paul had a gift, much like you." He let the door swing open on its own, still revealing the room much too quickly. He'd avoided this room at all costs since the memorial service. It reminded him of too many painful memories. Of his failure.

"Paul?"

"I don't know where he picked it up, exactly." He stepped aside so she could enter the room. He felt safest by the door.

"These are really good, Brantley."

"I know."

"No, I mean like *really* good."

He slid his hands into his jeans front pockets. "He mentioned something about a photography class or something when I first got to Alaska. Tried to get me to go with him, actually." Funny, the details he'd forgotten by simply avoiding contact with anything that conjured a memory.

"I bet that's what it was." Jillian lifted a print from the stack on the floor, one with a simple black wood frame. "Alaska. This one looks like it was taken up there." She turned, forcing him to look at the photo she picked up. One with snowcapped mountains, evergreen trees, and a caribou lurking in the middle distance.

"Could be." His throat felt tighter again. He didn't like it.

"Why haven't you done anything with these?" The question was innocent enough. Nothing in her tone implied a lecture or accusation. Merely idle curiosity. "These should be hung in a gallery or at least in places people could enjoy them."

"I don't like coming in here. It reminds me I wasn't there when he needed me most." At the first hint of watering eyes, he dipped out of the room. "I'm going to put on a pot of coffee."

He'd not shed a single tear since the day of the memorial service. He'd let out plenty prior, and he was done. Paul was gone, and no number of tears would bring him back.

He called back over his shoulder, "Close the door when you're done looking around."

Had Paul ever mentioned his plans when his sunrise photo project was complete? He thought back to the evening out at a bar and grill in Fairbanks when the conversation came up. Paul had successfully talked him out of volunteering for the deployment by then.

"A sunrise is such an amazing thing," Paul had

proclaimed. "Represents the beginning of so many things. I want to travel the country and get all the best sunrise shots."

"What are you going to do with them?"

He struggled to remember the conversation. Parts of it were blurry. Like Paul's answer to that question. Had he mentioned building a house and showcasing them that way? Or selling them?

"You should come with me," Paul had pressed on. "When I get back. We'll do it together."

Back then, the detail hadn't been all that important. Only the promise of a project they'd complete together. But now he wished he'd been listening better. He wished he knew what Paul wanted him to do with those photos now that they were left in his charge.

Even now, he wasn't sure why Paul had insisted his little brother, who had zero photography experience, come along on an extended trip to take photographs. But Brantley wanted his brother to be proud of him, so he agreed.

In the kitchen, he grabbed two mugs out of the cupboard and filled them. Jillian was still browsing the collection, and he wasn't about to rush her.

During the months leading up to the deployment that would signify the end of Brantley's service term and Paul's third trip overseas, he and Paul planned their route. They'd start with the Grand Canyon. Paul already had shots of Arches National Park, of

Zion, of Glacier. He'd gotten everything within a day's drive of home. "But I want more. I want to grab everything left on the west coast, then head east."

"How long you think this trip will take?"

"Three months at least. Maybe more."

Guilt pulled at him when he remembered the rooftop tent. He could finish Paul's project. Holly would let him take the time off. It would take Brantley more than three months since he'd have no one to share the driving. He could come back home after Christmas.

"Your brother was incredibly talented," Jillian said as she emerged from the room. Then, memories of that kiss invaded every other thought and suddenly, leaving Starlight not only seemed like a bad idea, it seemed an impossible one.

"He was."

"You should really consider doing something with those."

"I'll think about it. I promise." It occurred to him to tell her about the trip, but he couldn't bring himself to talk about it. He was barely holding it together as it was. Soon, he'd tell her everything. Maybe even get her input. But not tonight. "You'll still help me get the sunrise photo?"

She tapped the island counter with her nails, debate dancing in her eyes. "I wish you'd told me the truth from the get go. But yes, of course I'll still help you."

CHAPTER 17

Jillian

The ritzy hotel hosted the rehearsal dinner in an intimate space, much too small for Jillian's liking. Despite the lavish chandelier, organza tablecloths, and U-shaped table arrangement, this room felt too cramped and stuffy. There wasn't a single window. She wanted out.

"Isn't this fabulous?" Stella clapped her hands together at her exclamation, turning most of the half a dozen heads in the room. "Wait until you taste the sushi!"

She had to admit she'd expected a larger wedding party. It wouldn't be farfetched to image

Stella would want to string ten bridesmaids and ten groomsmen at the front of the ceremony area. But aside from her and Holly, the only other bridesmaid was the maid of honor, Stella's younger sister, Shelby.

Unfortunately, with Rodney's lack of brothers, Stella's nephew made the cut for the groomsmen. He sat on the other side of Stella's sister, head bent over his phone.

"Don't suppose we have alternatives?" Holly leaned in and whispered to her. "For those of us who don't do the whole sushi thing?"

"Sorry." Holly would starve before she touched sushi.

"It's okay." She patted Jillian's arm. "You still owe me that steak."

"Jillian!" She had hoped Stella's smug nephew Chad wouldn't remember her. It was wishful thinking at best. Especially since Stella had tried so desperately to get the two together yesterday. But apparently he not only found a moment to break away from his phone, but to also get up and walk halfway around the U-shaped tables. "How've you been?"

To the unsuspecting victim, Chad was charming, incredibly attractive, charismatic. He usually had a posse of fans of the female variety fawning around him. But it took about five minutes of him running his mouth to turn the smart ones away.

"Life is pretty amazing. I actually—"

"Great, great." And there it was, the polite question immediately followed by an interruption. Because Chad only cared about one individual: himself. "Stella told me about your interest in photography. Thought you might like to spend some one-on-one time together." He winked.

Her stomach knotted.

"I might be willing to share my secrets with you."

"Secrets?" Jillian felt as if she'd swallowed a glass of sour milk.

Brantley wrapped his arm around the back of her chair, his hand resting possessively on her shoulder. "Do you own your own business?" he asked.

"I work for the biggest photography chain in Philadelphia. Have my own corner office." Chad had probably mastered his smug smile at age ten. She wondered if his facial muscles knew how to form any other expression. She didn't think they'd remember how.

"Jilly here owns her own business. Isn't that something?" He played with the loose hairs at the base of her neck, sending shivers throughout her body. "She's got amazing talent. Maybe she can give you some pointers to take back to Philadelphia?"

"P-pointers?"

What amount of money would she have paid to see Chad speechless as he was now? A smirk formed on her lips, and she didn't care if Chad saw it. In fact, she hoped he did. "I'm sure you're far too busy this weekend, but if you change your mind, let me know."

Confusion settled, replacing the arrogance. Chad's face showed he didn't know how to respond, and the result was quite comical. "Better grab my seat." He winked at Holly on his way back to the empty chair beside Stella, and Holly nearly spit out her ice water.

"What a charmer." Brantley's deep voice came close to her ear, his breath causing strands of hair to tickle the base of her neck. He was putting on quite the act tonight, if the shocked reaction from Stella at the head of the table was any indication. Had she expected her nephew to sweep her off her feet and steal her away from Brantley?

"Can you imagine an entire week stuck around him?"

"Was that before or after he got his corner office?" Holly chimed in, reminding her that she and Brantley weren't alone.

Stella *tinked* her fork against a wine glass, though in this cramped room, there wasn't much point. "I'd like to thank you all for coming tonight." She dug into her purse and pulled out a stack of papers.

"Is she going to read that?" Holly whispered to her.

She could only shrug.

"I have a list of everything we need to accomplish tonight and through the reception tomorrow. I made copies so everyone knows what they need to do." She flagged down one of the servers and shoved a stack of hot pink lists into his hands. "Pass those out, please." The poor kid, hardly old enough to drive, stammered in his place. "Go on now, everyone needs a copy."

Jillian was through being surprised by Stella. The entire time she was in town, she'd been doing this—expecting everyone else to bend over backward for any want or need that might arise. She had told her time and time again how busy her schedule was. Outside of the blatant lie, Stella acted as if her business didn't matter. As though it wasn't a business at all.

Holly nudged her with her elbow, lifting the cardstock printed list at her. "Oh, you're not going to like this."

"What?" Brantley asked.

"She paired you with Chad."

Jillian sucked in a breath before looking down at the glittery list. She'd indeed be walking down the aisle with Chad. But it was more than that. Stella had assigned them a task together. Together alone. "Unbelievable." She kept her voice low, but her tone at least caught her dad's attention from across the room.

"Finalizing the reception playlist with the DJ?" Holly shook her head. "Don't worry, I'll help you. I'm not leaving you alone with him."

"You can't," Brantley said, reading the list. "You have to pick up tables and chairs with me. In Gillette."

"This is a *hotel*," Holly fired back. "They have *all* that stuff or they wouldn't be listed as a wedding venue."

She was certain that whatever the hotel had, Stella decided it wasn't good enough. She scooted her chair back, prepared to dart. This was too much. She loved her dad, but this was asking way more of her than she could stomach.

It was one thing to assume your future step-daughter was willing to lend a hand on the several demanded tasks. But quite another to assume she wanted to be set up with another guy when she already had a boyfriend.

Jillian dropped the list onto the table, her eyes darting to Stella.

Unless she knew.

"What's wrong?" Brantley asked.

Her heart rate shot through the roof. How on earth would Stella know the truth? She hardly ventured into town, and even then, the prospect of running into someone who knew her or Brantley well enough to know they weren't together was slim.

"Jilly."

"I think she knows."

He followed her eyes. "Stella."

"Yeah." She scanned the room. Did she recognize any of the servers? Had one of them tipped Stella off? The seamstress had never met Jillian before the dress fitting. One by one, Jillian eliminated different possibilities.

"How?"

The answer hit her so quickly she wasn't ready for the punch it packed. "Peggy."

"From the flower shop?"

"Kiss me."

"What?"

"Please. Whatever she thinks, we've got to convince her it's not true. Kiss me. Quick!"

Brantley pulled her closer with his arm around her shoulder. "I'm not going to do that, Jilly."

"Why not?"

"Because what you're asking for wouldn't even look real." Brantley traced a finger down her jawline, turning her face slowly toward his. "If we do this, we need it to look convincing, not staged."

"R-right." Her eyes fell to his lips, and the heated memories of their last kiss made her suddenly nervous. It was all pretend, but her body seemed not to have gotten that message.

With the tip of his finger beneath her chin, he drew her in slowly. The room around them faded away. She couldn't quite remember where they were or what they were doing. Her heart was too busy thundering in her ears.

Brantley brushed a soft, sweet kiss on her lips. She melted.

His finger dropped and he sat back at another *tink* of the glasses. "That was better than what you had in mind, no?"

Breathless, all she could do was nod.

———

It was only by a miracle that Jillian survived the rehearsal dinner. Holly'd been a genius conjuring up a seafood reaction bit to get her out of the bachelorette celebration Stella had planned. Holly hadn't wanted to go any more than she had.

"She's certifiably insane," Holly decided after dinner.

"Tell me about it."

They headed, per instruction, downtown to meet the DJ. Holly volunteered to stay and help her once her stomach began to feel queasy. The excuse worked to shove Chad with Brantley on a drive to Gillette. Jillian would need to make something extra special for breakfast tomorrow in thanks.

"This takes Bridezilla to a whole new level. Since we're done with the DJ, let's go home."

"In twenty-four hours, they should be headed to the airport." She gripped the seat belt across her chest as though it might somehow absorb her stress.

"I don't know why I didn't agree to go to Cancun. Surely it couldn't be any worse than this."

"Oh, I think it could."

She invited Holly in for a glass of wine. If the wedding weren't tomorrow, they'd finish off the bottle. One day soon, they'd have to celebrate surviving this nightmarish week.

"I want to see those photos," Holly demanded once her glass was filled with the gas station's finest chardonnay. "That little run-in with that Chad fellow makes me want to plan your entire successful future and the empire you're going to build."

Milo barked in agreement, tail wagging.

Jillian had no more than sat at her computer when Holly spotted the photo of Brantley and Milo. Dang it, if she hadn't been running so behind, she would have dropped it off at Brantley's before the rehearsal dinner and Holly wouldn't have a wide-open opportunity to pry.

"Brantley seemed pretty possessive of you tonight. I think he was jealous."

"Of Chad? That was show."

"The guy's a little conceited, but he's not bad on the eyes."

"Holly!"

"*I'm* not going after him." She looked around the desk, most likely for projectiles that could be aimed at her, but when she found nothing more than that photo, she relented. "I think there's more going on here than this fake relationship."

Back at the reception hall in the hotel, she had confessed her worries to Holly that Stella might know. That Peggy might've let slip without realizing what she did. "I don't get why she hasn't confronted me yet." Except, she feared Stella was aiming for the ultimate insult: public humiliation.

Why, she couldn't figure out.

"I don't think she hates you," Holly said. "I just think she's a little . . . high maintenance."

They spent an hour going over the Livingston photos, discussing potential business opportunities for her. "You should take photos of the ranch, too," Holly suggested. "You can tag along for any of it as long as you don't get in the way. If you don't want to ride a horse, you can take an ATV. That way you'll have photos to showcase on your website."

One day, she would get back on a horse on her own. Soon, she promised herself.

Holly left when her glass of wine was depleted and they were both fighting a fit of yawns. "I wonder if Brantley and Chad made it back from Gillette with all those tables and chairs."

She eyed the photo of Brantley and Milo propped on the desk. "Let me drop you off," she said to Holly. She slipped the photo into her purse when her friend wasn't looking.

. . .

Brantley wasn't home yet. Poor guy had probably gotten roped into unloading and setting up those tables and chairs. She wondered if Chad had suffered the same fate, or if Stella rescued him from any manual labor. She'd be furious once she learned her itinerary wasn't followed to the letter.

Jillian almost didn't stop, but she decided to try the front door. Maybe he left it unlocked and she could leave the photo inside.

The knob rattled, but refused to budge. Made sense. Even on a ranch one could never be too careful. She looked around, thinking she might find a spare key and spotted the mailbox near the front door instead. Jillian fished the five-by-seven photo out of her purse and slipped it in, sandwiching it between a magazine and a padded envelope.

Back in her car, she shot Brantley a text.

Jillian: How's the drive?
Brantley: Not so bad. Got invited to The Watering Hole later to meet Hudson. You should come.
Jillian: Maybe

Was it a good idea to meet Brantley in town tonight? That kiss, so much more potent than the first, still made her toes curl. With anyone else, a simple, soft kiss like that had never had that kind of effect on her.

She knew something was wrong when she neared her cabin. A vehicle she didn't recognize was parked outside. At first, she thought it might be Brantley and Chad, but a closer look revealed someone completely unexpected.

Her heart dropped into her toes.

Dad.

Twenty-four hours. That was all she had left in this week-long wedding nightmare. Twenty-four more hours to keep her dad and Stella away from her studio. She craned her neck to see inside the truck before getting out of her own car. No Stella.

"Dad, what are you doing here?"

"This is it?" Rodney, stationed outside the driver's side door of his rental truck, nodded toward the cabin. "This is your photography studio?"

Jillian's first instinct was to lie. To fabricate some elaborate story about how her building was under renovation and Holly had been nice enough to let her set up a temporary shop here. But her heart twisted as she recalled her mom's advice.

"Yes. This is it."

"Stella tried telling me, but I didn't believe her. Said she found your place on the Internet. That it looked nothing like what you said."

Stella. Always Stella. She seethed inside, unable

to hold back her outburst. "Of course Stella found it. She has it out for me."

Rodney hadn't moved from his spot, hadn't unfolded his arms. The dusky evening hid most of his expression, but she knew what was there. A disapproving, deepening scowl. "I *defended* you, Jillian."

Gone was the endearing nickname.

"If Stella hadn't made me feel—"

"We relocated our *wedding* for you. To accommodate your busy schedule. But word around town is hardly anyone has heard of you. How many clients have you really had this week?"

Bravely, Jillian took a step forward and hopped up the couple of steps onto her porch. "Two." She let out a defeated sigh. "You might as well come in and see the place." She wished she'd finished even a couple of the Livingston prints to hang in her studio. Something to add to the very bare collection on her walls.

"I've seen it."

She'd left the downstairs lights on, and curtains parted for Milo. One could easily peek through the windows and see everything there was to see. "I can show you what I've been working on."

"I don't think so." Rodney gripped the handle to the truck door. "I don't know what made you feel you had to lie—"

"You want to know why?" Jillian felt her anger

bubble again. Why couldn't her dad see that Stella was causing *all* of this? "It's Stella. Nothing I do is ever good enough for her approval. I don't even get why you're marrying her."

"Glad you have it all figured out." He sprang into the truck and slammed the door, leaving Jillian to crumble on the porch. "I'm gone."

"Fine. Go!"

"I thought you were sick from the sushi," he said out the window of his truck. "But you look awfully fine to me."

Her hands shook at her sides as her dad sped away, leaving a dust trail in his path. Inside, she was seething.

"Milo, why couldn't you be a big, bag guard dog tonight?" she said to the dog once inside. The dog tilted his head, like the thought intrigued him.

Her phone pinged in her pocket.

Brantley: You coming?

Her zooming heart rate slowly subsided. She needed to calm down.

A feeling of dread twisted in her stomach. She knew what had to be done. It was time to come clean. About everything.

CHAPTER 18

*B*rantley

The Watering Hole was the place to be in Starlight on any given weekend; still, Brantley was hopeful for a smaller crowd tonight. He yearned for the peace and quiet of the ranch, wishing he hadn't agreed to come out. The parking lot was a little fuller than he expected, forcing him to park along the curb a half block away and walk.

"Charming," Chad said on the way to the door. The exterior left a little something to be desired, or so city folks might think. The brick seemed a little washed and worn, the painted letters at the top of the second story could use a fresh coat, and the barrels of flowers needed weeding.

"They have the best wings in town." Country music played over the speakers as he slipped inside, searching for signs of his friend. He'd invited Hudson to join them so he wouldn't have to tolerate Chad alone. He had hoped to drop Chad off at the hotel and be done with him, but no such luck.

The last thing he expected to spend his Friday night doing was driving to Gillette with Stella's city slicker nephew. They'd driven the whole way only to find that the promised chairs and tables weren't available. Odd how Stella didn't seem in any kind of panic when he passed along that news.

If anything, she seemed more annoyed that he took Chad along instead of Holly.

"You really like living here?" Chad asked. Not to be insulting, he didn't think, but the idle curiosity of someone who'd never been within ten feet of a cow.

"It's home. Couldn't imagine living anywhere else." He had lived elsewhere, of course, but he didn't feel like bringing that up tonight. They found a table near the bar and sat at two of the four chairs.

He checked his phone again, hoping Jillian would respond. His mind raced, his senses heightened. The graze of her lips against his own would haunt him indefinitely if this blew up in his face. In less than a day, their need to fake a relationship would be gone. Where would that leave them?

"You and Jill, you been a thing for a while?"

"Jillian," he corrected. Had Stella started an

epidemic or something with this Jill business? Sometimes he thought she was naive enough and completely unaware of her overbearing nature. Other times, he couldn't help but wonder whether she was getting even with Jillian for bailing on the Cancun wedding. He'd known some spiteful people in his day; he hadn't decided whether Stella was one of them. "Two years."

It was an odd sort of Friday night. No live bands, no karaoke competitions or pool tournaments. Just a quiet crowd having a couple of drinks.

"It's funny," Chad said, "because I could have sworn she told me your name was Jason. You know, when we spent a week together last summer."

Ah, *that* trip. After two hours stuck in a truck with Chad, he could understand why Jillian lied to Chad about having a boyfriend. He flagged down a waitress. "Definitely not a Jason."

"Brantley!" Corrine rubbed his shoulder. Of course she was working tonight. He should have realized that possibility when Chad asked about a place to grab a drink. But any other bar in town was a few notches below The Watering Hole and didn't always have the most desirable crowds. Though he wouldn't be upset to see Chad overstep with his strongly opinionated ways, he was certain Rodney and Stella would prefer him not to have a busted lip or black eye tomorrow. "Who's your friend?"

He shrugged her hand off his shoulder, her

familiar strong perfume nearly making him sneeze. "Corrine Daily, meet Chad—"

"Chad Jenkins."

Good. With the way Chad's eyes zoned in on her, he hoped the two of them would hit it off and leave him alone. He didn't need the complications Corrine might invite to the evening.

He ordered a beer. He and Corrine both waited as Chad reached for a drink menu and took his time deciding. "Bring him a beer, too. If he doesn't drink it, I will."

"Oh, I can give the man a minute to decide," Corrine cooed at him, her attention moving over his right shoulder. Well, maybe he wouldn't be lucky enough after all. Chad seemed more interested in the object of Corrine's attentions.

"You fellows have room for one more?" Rodney Harper pulled out a chair and plopped down. The lines on his face seemed more defined, as though he might be more stressed about tomorrow's wedding than he wanted to let on. "Can I get a scotch on the rocks?"

"You got it." Corrine turned her attention back to Chad. "We have an excellent selection of whiskey if you're a whiskey kind of man."

"Tonight, I can be anything you want."

Rodney and Brantley looked at each other from across the table, as if to say *this guy for real?* But then

Rodney's expression settled into a deep scowl. Brantley felt a little uneasy at what it might mean.

"I'll bring you something good." She patted Chad on the shoulder as she turned for the bar to put in the order. Chad was probably getting a glass of their most expensive whiskey. The thought made him smirk. Let the man overpay for a few drinks. She was a flirt, but not one to entertain unwanted attention. In the end, Corrine always came out on top.

"You look a little worse for wear there, Mr. Harper," he said cautiously, hopeful to gain some insight before he stuck his foot in his mouth.

He lifted his eyes from a menu he'd been holding upside down. With Chad on his phone, already tuned out of the conversation, Rodney answered, "Been an interesting evening."

Something in that weary tone had him on high alert. He wanted to ask about the wedding, but with Stella's nephew sitting right beside them, he didn't dare. All he needed was that weasel going back to his aunt and spreading rumors about calling the wedding off. But maybe the tone was about Jillian.

"Here you go." Corrine served the drinks and asked about appetizers. Only Chad seemed hungry, judging by the loaded nacho plate he ordered. Again, she rested her arm on Brantley's shoulder. "You boys need anything else right now?"

"That should do it." He shrugged her hand off

again, but she dug her fingers into his shoulder blade and held on.

Instead of leaving them, she leaned down and said, "You never called me." She'd quieted her voice, but not enough for the country music to drown it out. Across the table, Rodney's frown deepened.

"Didn't know you expected me to." He knew how bad this looked. Whether the rumors about him and Jillian had gotten back to Corrine was uncertain. But if they had, they hadn't deterred her at all. If he wasn't careful, she might spill everything right now. She might buy that he and Jillian were dating, but not for two years. She'd wouldn't be shy about saying so in front of everyone, either.

She put on that pouty face. One that usually got her what she wanted with any other man. "You even have my number?"

"Nope." He failed again to shrug free of her grip and was forced to stand instead. "I bet your new buddy Chad would like it, though." He wove his way through the growing crowd toward the back door near the restrooms. He needed some air. He needed to call Jillian and warn her something was off. Ask her if something happened with her dad.

The evening had brought with it a refreshing breeze. He let the door close behind him and leaned against the side of the building. Around the other side was a deck overlooking the river where a large majority of the crowd sat, unaware of his presence.

He pulled out his phone. Still no response from Jillian. Before he could type out another text, the door opened.

"Mind filling me in?" Though the darkness hid Rodney's face, Brantley had little doubt it was beet red. The man wasn't built of muscle, but he was a couple of inches taller than Brantley. And when it came to protecting his daughter, he could probably pack a good punch.

"There's nothing going on with that waitress," he told him, not sure Rodney believed it. "She's been chasing me since I moved back home, and she won't take no for an answer. Come in any day of the week and it's the same old game with her."

Folding his arms tightly across his chest, Rodney stood inches from him, facing him. "Do you love my daughter?"

"Very much." He didn't have to think on that answer, because it was the truth. Fake relationship or not, he would always love Jillian Harper. His blessing or his curse, he wasn't sure yet.

"You mean that?"

"I've been in love with your daughter since the first day I saw her."

"That would explain you covering for her," Rodney muttered.

He didn't like that his suspicions were right, but he wouldn't admit guilt without knowing how much Rodney knew. "Jilly showed up at the stable on my family's ranch in cowgirl boots and an oversized plaid shirt. She'd never been near a horse in her life. Certainly didn't expect at fifteen to be shoveling out their stalls. But she had a spunk about her that stuck with me. She never gives up."

"My Jillian?" Something in Rodney's tone softened a notch.

"Yes, sir."

"I couldn't get her to go near a horse."

He knew she hadn't started working on the ranch until after her dad left. She'd been very bitter about it that summer, convinced she had to work because her mom couldn't afford to pay for everything now that they were on their own. Later, her mom told her it was because she wanted her to have a backbone.

"She's great with horses. Took her out riding the other day. My great aunt has a horse she can't ride anymore. I thought Jilly was going to steal Buttercup and take her home."

"Why haven't you bought her a ring yet?" Rodney asked.

The question caught him off guard. That kind usually came from Stella. "I have." He'd saved up his money from his time in the military and bought her a beautiful diamond weeks before he packed up for the drive home to Wyoming. He hadn't planned to ask right away. No, but he *had* planned to make her fall in love with him so when the time was right, he already had the perfect ring.

"What're you waiting for?"

He didn't know how to answer that question honestly. He couldn't tell Rodney that he still had to work on the 'getting Jillian to fall in love with him' part. And it would take more than a week and a fake relationship to accomplish it. So he went with another angle.

"I have something I might need to do first."

"What's that?"

Since he'd been talking about his brother all week, it was a little easier now without choking up or feeling his chest tighten. He told Rodney about the trip he and Paul never got to take. "Jillian's been teaching me to take photographs. They'll never be as good as Paul's were, but I still think it might be a good tribute to my brother if I finish what he started."

"You'd be gone a while."

"Probably three or four months. Maybe a little more."

"You should do it," Rodney said. "You'll feel restless if you don't. My daughter doesn't deserve someone who isn't ready to settle down."

Although the topic had arisen only as a way to excuse the proposal he hadn't made yet, there was truth in those words that resounded a little too loudly. He wished he had more time with Jillian to learn about lighting and angles, but Paul had a journal filled with notes. "I don't know, maybe."

"Thought about asking her to go with you?"

"What?" Although her photography studio hadn't exactly been booked weeks out, Jillian had been scheduling more clients. She'd bragged about another new one earlier at the rehearsal dinner. Someone Violet had no doubt sent her way. And her classes were in high demand, from what he heard. He couldn't possibly ask her to come with him and risk losing all the new business she was drumming up.

"Tell you what. Stella was never going to let me buy that rooftop tent for myself. She's right, too. I wouldn't use it. She might be a little much for some people, but she's good for me. Knows me better than I know myself most days." He reached for the back door, pulling it open. "But I could buy one for you."

"I couldn't let you—"

"I'm not asking." Rodney clapped him on the shoulder. "If you really do love Jillian as much as you say, go finish your trip. Take her with you if she'll go. When you get back, give her that ring." He slipped back inside, leaving Brantley alone with the biggest decisions of his life.

 illian

The second the back door at The Watering Hole pulled free from her hold, Jillian skittered away and hid in the ladies' restroom. She'd missed part of the conversation, she realized in frustration. Only heard something about her dad buying Brantley a rooftop tent.

But the question remained, why had Brantley never told her about his desire to finish the trip? It was obviously something important to him, if the passion in his voice as he told her dad about it was any indication.

This changed everything.

She'd arrived ten minutes before to find Chad alone at a table, scrolling through Facebook like he was looking for someone. When she asked, he pulled the phone away. "I don't know where they went," he said. "Restroom maybe?"

Unwilling to sit alone with Chad for any length of time, she wandered into the back hallway to find the door ajar. Her first instinct had been to close it to keep the bugs out. But then she heard voices. Brantley's it turned out, talking about his brother and the epic trip they planned.

She realized earlier that night how she felt about him. That she loved him. Maybe she had for a while, but it had taken a couple of kisses to no longer lie to herself. She wasn't sure what would happen once the truth came out.

Brantley would be off the hook for the wedding.

On her drive over, she considered confessing her true feelings. Her dad already knew her photography business was a joke. It seemed all too likely that Stella had shared her suspicions on their relationship, too. Why not go for broke?

But if Holly and her mom were right and Brantley did have feelings for her, telling him might hold him back from this trip. An ode to his brother. Brantley had finally opened up about Paul after more than a year of silence. He needed to do this now or he'd likely never go. She wished she'd spent more time this week preparing him. They could have worked on lighting, framing, editing.

She cowered in the bathroom for a few minutes before sneaking out the back door of the restaurant. She'd face everyone soon enough. But first, she needed to make a call.

Her mom answered on the second ring. "I don't need to help you hide any dead bodies, do I?"

Though it would be impossible to feel completely relieved tonight, she did feel a smidge better hearing her mom's voice. Selfishly she wished she'd begged her to make the trip. But her mom didn't have the funds, and she didn't either.

She was done being selfish. It would likely be torture for her mom to be here this weekend anyway. "No dead bodies."

"You ready for the wedding tomorrow?"

"If I'm still invited."

"Uh-oh. What happened?"

"Stella." The word fell out of her mouth before she even had time to think. Sure, Stella had been smart enough to figure out the lies. But she realized on her drive into town that Stella wasn't the real problem. "She figured out that I'm not a super successful, in-demand photographer. Dad came to see the studio, unannounced."

"Oh, dear."

"I might have said a few not-so-nice things about Stella." Jillian told her about the little episode outside her cabin, and how she learned her dad was at The Watering Hole too.

"Jilly Bean, you can't go back in time. All you can do is own up to the mess you've made and try to make it right."

Shoulders sinking, she leaned against the back of the building in defeat. "I was afraid you'd say that."

"You're on damage control now, honey."

She wanted Mom's advice about what to do about Brantley, especially with her newest knowledge that kept tearing at her heart. But that was something Jillian had already figured out for herself. She just didn't like the answer. "I'm telling them tonight. No more lies."

"Good. Good idea to clear the air before the wedding."

A wedding Jillian may not even be attending. That remained to be seen. "Thanks, Mom."

"Always, Jilly Bean."

Since she arrived and found Chad sitting alone at a table for four, others had appeared. They'd pulled over another table to accommodate everyone.

Instead of only Chad, her dad, and Brantley, a few more had joined the ranks to include Stella and her sister. Holly toasted her with her bottle of beer as she took a seat next to Brantley. Brantley's friend Hudson had joined the table, unfortunately stuck next to Chad. Had the man looked up from his phone even once since Jillian first got here? Maybe he didn't even know the crowd had grown.

"Glad you could make it out." Brantley's arm went around the back of her chair and she melted into the touch, the security it brought her. Just a few more minutes. That's all she needed before she shattered the fun with the horrid truth.

Her dad wouldn't look up. He rolled the ice cubes around his glass, eyes fixated on its movement.

"Jill, so wonderful to see you feeling better," Stella hollered from the opposite corner of the table. "You looked positively green after dinner."

"I'm fine now, thanks."

Holly ducked her head below Brantley's chin. "Everything okay?" she asked as discreetly as she could with a man between them.

She wished there'd been time to order a drink. She could use one before she made her embarrassing confession. The cowardly part of her wanted to wait until only her dad and Brantley remained. But she'd been lying long enough. If she waited, she'd lose her nerve. "Yes."

"I'm going to grab another round," Holly told her, grabbing Hudson to help carry the drinks. She smiled a thank you at her friend, wishing somehow she could get Chad away too.

With a deep breath, she studied the table. "I'm *not* Starlight's most in-demand photographer." She waited a moment to make sure she had everyone's attention. Even Chad looked up from his phone at that proclamation. "I don't have a fancy studio under renovation or clients booked out for months."

Brantley leaned in and whispered in her ear, "Jilly, what are you doing?" She met his eyes for a moment, pleading for him to trust her. She was afraid she'd hurt him most of all.

"I work out of a tiny cabin on the Maxwell Ranch. One I pay rent by doing chores. I live in a tiny apartment upstairs, smaller than most walk-in closets. I've had two clients this entire week, and one didn't book me. I have to work shifts at Mabel's to make sure I can keep the lights on."

Finally, her dad looked up. Though his stern expression hadn't changed, there was a softness in his eyes. Sympathy? Pity?

"Why the lies?" It took a beat, but that's what Stella asked.

She had to choke down the vile words that threatened to come up. Ones directed at the woman who'd be her stepmother in less than twenty-four hours. She reminded herself that Stella had never forced her to lie. That had been her own choice. "I wanted you to be proud of me, Dad."

"What about him?" Stella pushed, waving a hand at Brantley. "Is he a lie, too? Our waitress says you two aren't a couple. Says Brantley hasn't even been home from the military for two years. Is that true?"

Beneath the table, she curled her fingers around her thighs and squeezed. Stella might do this all night. She always jumped at an opportunity to humiliate, it seemed. *Why*, Jillian could hardly understand.

"Jilly, you don't have to—"

"Corrine is right," she said, cutting Brantley off. "We're not really dating. I asked him to pretend he was my boyfriend for the week."

"I don't understand," Rodney said, wrinkles on his forehead more prominent. "You talked about him when you visited last." She didn't miss that her dad's confused gaze fell on Brantley and stayed there.

"That was Jason," Chad offered, a smug smile on his face. He probably loved every second of this embarrassing episode since she had more than shot him down on a few occasions.

"Jason?" Rodney repeated.

"I was engaged to a man named Jason, who dumped me the day I opened my studio."

Jillian let the pieces fall together for her dad about the timing, ignoring the drawn eyebrows and confused expressions of the others at the table. "You never even told me you were engaged."

"I had planned to tell you when I visited. But the truth was too humiliating. Too fresh." She wanted to make a snide comment about Stella pushing Chad onto her, but she let it go. It would only make her feel better for a moment, and then everyone would feel terrible.

Brantley's hand rubbed her shoulder. She would miss that.

"Why did you RSVP no to the wedding in Cancun?" Rodney asked. "It was an all-expenses-paid trip."

"And you obviously weren't too busy," Stella chimed in, expression blank. But those eyes held some semblance of victory. Yes, she was sure Stella had gone out of her way to uncover the web of lies.

The truth almost fell out before she could catch it. This one-time lie was better, though. Stella was marrying her dad tomorrow whether she liked it or not. She didn't understand it, what Dad saw in the woman, but she wouldn't get in the way. "I couldn't stand the idea of going alone. Of going to any wedding, really." And then, truth crept in anyway. "This summer was supposed to be *my* wedding." She pushed back from her chair. "Excuse me."

She made it to the parking lot before Brantley caught up to her. She'd had to park two blocks away along the street. "Hey, wait up! Jilly!"

"You're off the hook, Brantley." She could hardly face him. She wanted him to wrap her in his arms, but she'd never be able to push him away if she let that happen. "You don't have to go the wedding tomorrow."

"What are you talking about? Of course I'll be there."

She shook her head, warding off tears. She couldn't allow herself to cry in front of Brantley. "No. Don't come."

The streetlight lit up the confusion in his eyes. "Jilly, I can still be your plus one to the wedding. I'm not going to make you face that alone."

"I don't even think I'm invited anymore." She started walking again, but Brantley caught up to her with a few brisk strides.

"Jilly, stop." His hand circled her wrist, and she found she didn't have much fight to stop him. Didn't want to get away so easily. "Look at me. Please."

She steeled herself, because she feared what was coming. Her heart cracked at what she was about to do.

"I love you, Jilly. I've *been* in love with you. I want us to be together, and not for some fake relationship. For real. Please, tell me you feel the same way. Tell me I'm not imagining everything that's happened the last few days."

Tears welled in her eyes. She couldn't go with him on his trip, yet if he knew how she felt, he'd stay and never go. "I'm sorry, Brantley. I'm so sorry."

His hands dropped to his sides at her words, and her heart split open at the pain in his eyes. "Tell me you don't love me."

It took every ounce of strength she had to look

him in the eyes and tell the only lie Brantley would ever believe. "I don't love you."

His lips parted, as if he might try one last plea. But they closed and he turned away. He made it a few steps before his head turned over his shoulder. "I was never pretending, Jilly. Not once."

She let him walk away, though it felt as if daggers stabbed into her heart to do so. This was the only way, she knew. The only way he'd take her dad up on his offer of the rooftop tent, and finish Paul's final project. If she didn't push him away, he'd find too many excuses to stay. He'd regret it.

Jillian had a glimmer of hope that he'd come back to her at the end of the trip, ready to forgive her for the biggest lie she'd told this entire week.

But it was a lot to hope for.

CHAPTER 20

*B*rantley

Brantley had been avoiding the cemetery since the funeral. If he were being honest with himself, he'd been avoiding a lot of things.

Standing outside the iron gate, looking in through the bars that towered over him, he felt trapped. Trapped from the outside. But Jilly's words whispered through his mind. *You need to go. Do this for Paul, but do it for yourself, too.*

He should be at a wedding right now, but Jillian had made it more than clear he wasn't needed anymore. She made it easy for him to make the hard decisions. But he couldn't leave town without first stopping by the cemetery.

Lifting the heavy latch, he let himself in to the well-maintained grounds. Crisp, bright grass filled the acres within those walls. Tall trees provided shade in thick patches. Maybe he should lock the gate behind him, but he wanted an easy escape if emotions became too heavy.

Each step felt like a mile-long march. Why hadn't he gone on that deployment? They had given him a choice, and he did what his brother told him to do. If only he'd gone, maybe he could have saved Paul. Maybe . . .

"Get out, get home," Paul said that night in Brantley's barracks room. "Hardly anyone gets the option, sport." *Sport*. The nickname his brother had used for years. Always made him feel like a kid. It was almost enough for him to say no, to prove to his brother he wasn't some kid anymore. Surely going to Afghanistan with him would finally prove that.

He almost went.

"The family needs one of us," Paul said, clapping him on the back. "They're hurting for help back at the ranch. Mom needs someone to look after her, too." A silent stare passed between them. Paul had hit on a point Brantley couldn't argue. The Maxwell family ranch had always meant something special to Brantley in ways it hadn't for Paul. He'd never intended to turn his back on it when he signed up for the Army. Hadn't thought they'd be hurting without him around.

"You think I should go home."

"You'll be happier on the ranch than in the desert. You and I both know that. You're needed back home."

He shuffled his way down a worn trail in the cemetery. It was the long way to Paul's grave, but he wasn't ready to arrive any sooner than he had to.

It was the promise that once Paul returned from Afghanistan, they'd travel the country together to wrap up Paul's sunrise photo project—that was what finally convinced him he could say no to the deployment. An option most soldiers were never given.

Despite the beautiful black granite headstone, it was the military marker that caught his eye first. The bronze plaque at the foot of the grave that wouldn't let him pull his eyes away. Suddenly he felt empty, gut punched at the overwhelming flood of emotions. He very much wanted Jillian at his side for comfort, but she made her feelings clear last night. She'd never see him as more than a friend.

He dropped to one knee, held the pose for a few minutes as he fought tears. Despite everything, he didn't want to cry. Not today.

"You're needed back home." It wasn't those words that haunted him in his dreams. No. It was the unspoken ones.

When he had gained enough of his composure, he relaxed into a sitting position on the dewy ground. "Well, Paul." He removed his hat and tossed it on the grass beside him. "It's been a minute." So many words he'd dreamt of saying over so many sleepless nights, but none wanted to come now.

"I'm going to do it. Picking up a rooftop tent of all things when I leave here. Already told Holly I'm taking the rest of the summer off from the ranch." He ran his hand through the soft blades of grass. The last time he was here, this spot had looked a lot different. "I'll never be anywhere near as good as you with the camera, but I'll give it my best shot."

He had already stopped at Edie's house, promised her Holly would be by two or three times a week to help with Buttercup. Hudson had offered too, help with repairs or chores that needed done around the property during his absence.

"You'll visit your mom?" Edie had asked.

"Yes, I promise." This time, he meant it. In fact, he'd already put it into his itinerary. Late last night, he'd selected a few prints to bring her, deciding he should have them framed before he got to Arizona. It was only right that she had a few of her own to display. To remind her of Paul, too.

He hoped most of all that spending a few months on the road would help him finally let go of the dream he'd held on to for so long. That he and Jillian were somehow destined to end up together. Letting it go was the only way he'd be able to return home and stay.

———

Jillian

It was only because Holly had texted her first thing this morning that Jillian knew she still had an invite to the wedding. Stella didn't want the visual appearance of her bridal party skewed by her absence, nor did she have anyone who could fit into the dress so last minute.

Holly met her at the hotel and they helped each other into the hot pink ruffle explosions Stella insisted on. She still hadn't decided whether Stella truly loved the dresses or if she loved how ridiculous they looked in them more.

"How was it after I left?" Jillian finally asked. The question had been burning all morning, but she hadn't felt up to asking until now.

"Awkward." Holly yanked on the zipper at the back of her dress and spun her toward the mirror. "No one said much of anything. Except Stella."

"No surprise there."

"And she had plenty to say." Holly pinned Jillian's hair into place, topping off the style with the matching pink bow. "Your dad shut her down, though."

"Really?"

"Yeah, shut everyone up when he finally did."

"What did he say?"

"A bunch of things. It mostly amounted to the fact that he loves his daughter no matter what."

"Oh." Jillian wanted to be more excited about that, but if her dad wasn't proud of her, well, she couldn't blame him.

"He wants you here today. Told Stella he wouldn't go through with the wedding unless his daughter was a part of it. Because you know she tried to conjure a replacement bridesmaid after you left."

"Shocking."

"What's in the bag?" Holly nodded to the black backpack dropped onto a chair in the corner.

"Camera."

"I thought you weren't taking photos."

"They didn't hire me," Jillian said, "but I thought I could grab some shots at the reception. Send them as an apology gift."

Holly gave Jillian a squeeze. "Good plan."

"Got to make things right where I can."

———

She couldn't help it. She kept glancing toward the ballroom's double-door entrance all through the reception. Holly told her at dinner that Brantley called to ask for the summer off. She'd been shocked to hear he left this morning, but not altogether surprised. She'd caused him so much pain.

"You really care about him, don't you?" Holly asked, following her eye trail toward the doors.

She reached for her champagne flute and took a sip. "That obvious, huh?"

"Why didn't you tell him the truth? I thought you were done lying." A cute man in a tuxedo winked at Holly and made his way across the dance floor. She wasn't sure whether he was a guest or a wedding crasher, but Holly didn't seem to mind.

"He would never have taken that trip. You know that."

Holly rested her hand on her arm. "I know you're right. Still sucks, though. I was sure you two would end up together."

"You were not!"

Holly winked, then met the cute man halfway for a dance.

"This seat taken?"

Rodney dropped into the chair Holly had vacated, and suddenly she didn't know what to say. Her palms grew a little sweaty. She'd met her dad's eyes a couple of times throughout the day, but they hadn't spoken since last night at The Watering Hole.

"Hi, Dad."

"I'm glad you came, Sweet Pea."

She turned in her chair to face him, covering his hand with her own. "You're sure you're happy, Dad?" It might be a little late to be asking, but she had to know the truth. "With Stella?"

"I know she's a little much at times. More high maintenance than anyone I've ever met. But heaven help me, I love the woman." Rodney's eyes lingered on his bride across the dance floor, spinning a little girl around with her. "She's taken good care of me."

"You don't mind the salads? Being retired?"

"Job was causing me an enormous amount of stress. Doctor suggested I retire. Suggested a lot of things. I didn't listen."

Stella.

"I'm sorry she's been a little harsh on you. It's her way of looking out for me. One of my colleagues was stealing my best clients, and when Stella got wind of that . . ." Rodney adjusted his tie until it loosened and pulled it free. "Let's just say she's a little protective of my interests. She didn't like being lied to. I didn't either."

"I'm sorry, Dad. Really, I am."

"I'm proud of you, Sweet Pea. You own your own business, and from what your friend tells me, you've been booking new clients all week."

"I have." She smiled, excited at the prospects of her future in photography. She was nearly giddy about the shots she captured in secret at the reception, too. She'd work on editing them right away.

"I ran into an old friend last night after you left. Wanted to mention an opportunity for you."

She stiffened out of instinct. Her dad had known a lot of people and done a lot of different things. She couldn't imagine forfeiting her photography business to pursue something else that simply paid the bills.

"A buddy of mine from when I lived here, turns out he's the editor of the *Starlight Gazette* now. Vince is his name. Said they're looking for a freelance photographer. I know it's not exactly what you dreamed up, but it might be something better than working diner shifts when you'd rather be taking photos." Rodney pulled a card out of his inner tuxedo pocket. "Give him a call Monday if you're interested."

She threw her hands around her dad and hugged him tight. "Thank you, Dad."

"Anything for my Sweet Pea." He pushed back from the chair, but before he got up, added, "I know you told everybody the whole thing with Brantley was fake, but that boy wasn't faking a thing. He loves you."

CHAPTER 21

Jillian

"Jillian, these are gorgeous!" Violet Livingston clapped her hand over her mouth, her eyes tearing with emotion. "The ones you emailed me were wonderful, but I never expected anything like this. In print, they're simply stunning!" She flipped through the photos again, slower this time. "You captured the very essence of this place. Of the people."

"I'm so glad you like them." She wanted to remain calm, but truth be told, this was the first moment of excitement she'd felt since Brantley left town almost two weeks ago. Everything felt emptier without him here. "They were Brantley's idea."

"Sounds like he was onto something. I hear you're booked for a handful of ranch shoots."

"I am."

"Have you heard from him?" Violet asked.

Jillian shook her head. She hadn't expected to. Several times since his departure she'd been tempted to send him a text. But it wasn't fair of her to do that.

"Ah, well, I hope everything is working out for him."

Her heart ached, not knowing whether he was having a good trip or if it was hard for him to be on the road without his brother. Even if she knew, though, she couldn't comfort him. Not after the way she broke his heart. "Me, too."

She accepted Violet's offer of pie. Only a fool turned down fresh lemon meringue made by the best baker in town.

"We might have you come back out," Violet said, joining her at the table. "We have a lot of different events throughout the year, you know. Calving, branding, just to name a couple. Even the day-to-day is important."

"I'd love to come back." She couldn't have hidden her smile if she tried. Having Violet Livingston interested in her shoots, wanting her to come back, it was a huge step in the right direction where the future of her business was concerned.

"You should focus your marketing efforts on this." Violet took a bite of pie. "Your website is too geared toward other things."

"I'm not sure how to advertise such a service. I don't know how many ranchers would want a photographer tagging along." Especially one who was still working on her fear of riding in the saddle. She'd tried a couple of times since Brantley left, but she hadn't lasted long, even when Holly suggested she come along with her to Edie's and ride Buttercup.

"Use your photos. They speak for themselves."

————

Brantley

It'd been two weeks on the road, traveling to the various locations on Paul's list on a roundabout route to Phoenix.

He spent three days at Yellowstone, because no matter how hard he tried, he kept screwing up the sunrise shots. Not only were they nowhere near as good as Paul's, they were frankly total crap. Someone with a smartphone could probably take a better one.

He hadn't warned his mom he was coming. He wanted the flexibility and the opportunity to escape quickly should he find himself not welcome. But it might be possible to find a photography class in Phoenix to help him out. At this rate, he'd have to revisit three places he already stopped at and retake those photos. His weren't worthy to sit beside Paul's works of art.

His mom had texted him her address shortly after their last call, asking to consider coming for a visit soon.

As he pulled into the driveway of a stucco ranch house with a seven-foot saguaro cactus in the front yard, he felt the familiar tightening of his chest. The last memory of his mom was at the funeral luncheon, with tear-streaked cheeks. Him numb and still in shock. They'd clung to each other that day, but she never once told him she was packing up the house and leaving days later. He had no warning.

His mom was in the driveway before he even got out of his Jeep. "Brantley?"

"Hi, Mom." He let the door fall closed and braced himself for the hug she attacked him with.

"You came."

"I'm here."

"Come, come inside."

The first few minutes were awkward, as to be expected. But once he retrieved Paul's framed prints in offering, the conversation went from slow and uncomfortable to voracious and lively. They talked for hours about their memories of Paul, emptying a half bottle of wine. They laughed, then cried.

"I'm finishing it, Mom. Paul's trip. The one we were going to do together. That's what I've been doing the last couple of weeks."

"Interesting." She was interrupted by the doorbell. They'd decided to order a pizza to save them both the trouble of figuring out dinner neither had the energy nor desire to prepare.

"I'm terrible at it, too."

"Of course you are. You're a rancher, not a photographer. You know how to fix things, to take care of horses and cattle, repair buildings and fences. Those were things Paul was no good at." She set the pizza box on the table and carried over a couple of plates. "You'll never be as good as Paul was with the camera, and that's okay."

"I feel like I'd be letting him down if I didn't at least try."

"You're not letting him down." She took her seat again. "You're sharing his prints with the people who love them. Letting them sit in a closed-off bedroom for a year because they reminded you too much of the pain, *that* was letting him down."

Her words sounded eerily familiar to Jillian's. She tried convincing him to display Paul's photos where people could enjoy them. Perhaps that *was* the real treasure. "The trip though. I thought that was finally something we were going to do together. As brothers."

"I want you to stay for a few days. But after that,

go home, Brantley. There was a reason Paul talked you out of that deployment. He knew how important Starlight was to you. If you'd gone overseas, you might never have gotten out of the Army at all. You might've spent your whole life trying to make up for something you had no control over in the first place."

His mom was right. He would probably have reenlisted like Paul's best friend had. He might never have gotten out. He'd done his time, and he was proud of that. But his heart always pulled him back to Wyoming.

Jilly, too.

His heart twisted at that, and he found he needed a minute.

"I think I left something in the Jeep." He slipped out the front door easily enough. Though he'd already brought in the prints and his bags, he had a pile of mail on his passenger seat that he'd grabbed in haste on his way out of town. Mostly junk, he knew but he'd failed to look through it. Right now, it gave him something to do.

He thumbed through the credit card offers, the lower insurance rate offers, one postcard from the dentist. But it was the single photo that slipped out of the pile and gently landed on his passenger seat that stopped him.

It was a picture of Milo, with him on the front porch of Jillian's cabin. He remembered that moment well, but had no idea she'd been sneaking around with a camera. She was in such a hurry to get to the diner.

He ached to text her. To call her so he could hear her voice.

"You got a dog?"

He knew his mom would follow him outside eventually, but she still managed to sneak up on him.

"No, that's Jillian's. Milo's his name."

"You two look awfully friendly."

"Yeah."

"How is Jillian Harper these days?"

He shrugged. "Don't know." He'd fought any and all urges to ask Holly how she was, much as he had while he lived in Alaska. He didn't want to know if she'd found someone new. Or *when*, as his luck seemed to have it. His heart could only break so many times.

"Heard quite the story about you two."

"You did?"

"Edie."

He nodded. "Of course." He should give his great aunt a call, make sure Holly and Hudson were seeing to her needs. He should probably take his mom's advice. Go back home. But he wasn't ready to face the woman who'd shattered his heart. The photo of Milo reminded him how much bite that pain had.

"You're welcome to stay a week," Mom said. "But then I'm off on another adventure. Bahamas this time. I'll have to kick you out then."

"A week?"

She patted him on the shoulder. "Pizza's cold now, just the way you like it. Don't be too long?"

He watched her disappear into the house, but his feet refused to move from his spot on the driveway. Something about that photo nagged at him, as though it contained a secret message. He flipped it over, hopeful to find a caption, a note, a date, something. But Jillian hadn't written a thing.

He dropped it onto the passenger seat, but a light breeze carried it onto the driveway. He rushed to pick it up before it blew under the Jeep, or worse, down the street. He didn't want to lose this piece of Jillian. This photo, taken with so much love and care.

Love.

Was it possible? His chest tingled at the very thought. Jillian had a gift, no one would argue. But this photo, taken when she was already late for her shift at the diner, it meant something more. He studied it closer. "Milo buddy, I think she loves me."

CHAPTER 22

Almost a month had gone by, and still Jillian missed Brantley. She might've missed him more during the time she spent at Edie's. The two had become well acquainted since she started coming over to help with Buttercup.

"I was bucked off a horse once, too," Edie told her one afternoon over coffee. "Scared me half to death. Broke my arm, twisted my ankle. Swore I'd never get on one again."

Jillian had lucked out when Timmy bucked her. No broken bones or serious injuries. Just a lot of scrapes and hurt pride. "How did you get over that?"

"Took a lot of time, and some help from Frank. He was supportive, never too pushy. But he also didn't let me back down. One day, I just decided enough was enough. I slipped out of the house while he was taking a nap and got back on. Didn't let my mind think I couldn't do it. Never had a problem since."

"Maybe today is that day for me."

Edie let her saddle Buttercup and walk her into the pasture toward the trails. She did this often enough, walking by Buttercup's side. But today she was going to ride. She had to.

"Alright Buttercup, I'm trusting you now." She stilled her nerves and wildly beating heart. Buttercup wouldn't care too much for all that. She focused on forcing all thoughts of her bad experience out of her mind. She imagined herself on the horse, riding and smiling. Another of Edie's suggestions.

In one swoop, she mounted Buttercup with ease. She didn't give herself time to think before urging the horse into a trot, and off they went.

They rode for nearly an hour, taking the trail Brantley showed her more than a month ago. She stopped for a break at his sunrise spot, thinking as she often did that she might come out here one morning and capture it. She didn't know when he'd be home, but Holly had a key to his cabin and could leave the picture inside for him.

Jillian was laughing as they trotted back, gleeful

at the joy of being on the back of a horse again without fear. Once she started working on a ranch all those years ago, she'd ridden constantly. She'd missed this so much. She had Brantley to thank for giving her the courage to ride again, even if he didn't know it.

When they reached the barn, her breath caught. Brantley's Jeep sat parked in the driveway. She frantically searched the area to locate him, but without success. He was back, though. After only a month.

Or was it simply a pitstop?

She dismounted Buttercup and walked her slowly to the pasture, much too close to the house now that Brantley might be sitting inside. The full branches of the mature trees made it hard to see everywhere.

It'd haunted her, the lie she told him that night outside The Watering Hole. It might be selfish, but she'd wanted to tell him that she loved him. Had even planned the way she'd tell him on her way over to meet him. Then she overheard the conversation with her dad about Paul's trip. She knew she'd have to let him go.

"Jilly?"

Brantley stood on the porch, and his eyes widened to see her walking Buttercup.

"Hey, Brantley."

"Did I really just see you riding?"

"Guilty." She removed the saddle, then opened

the pasture gate to let Buttercup roam free. She hadn't prepared herself to see Brantley until at least the end of the summer. Carrying everything back to the barn would buy her some time.

"I'm glad to see you got over your fear."

She spun around inside the barn, running the saddle into a post. It pushed her back a couple of steps and almost into Brantley. *Fear?* So he knew. "You're back sooner than I expected."

"Yeah." He took a few steps closer and helped lift the saddle to put it up. "I've been gone long enough, don't you think?"

"Did you make it to a lot of places?"

"A few." He stepped closer still once their hands were free, not leaving much distance between them.

"How about the photos?"

"They're terrible."

"Oh."

His fingers brushed away the stray strands of hair from her face. "I've always loved you with your hair down. But you never wear it that way anymore." His fingers worked the hair tie holding her hair back in a messy bun, undoing it with ease. Wavy locks fell around her shoulders. "Better. So much better."

"I stopped. After . . ."

"He was a fool." His fingers trailed her jawline, tipping her chin up toward him. "I know you lied, Jilly."

"You do?" Her voice came out as more of a squeak than anything.

"It was the picture." Brantley drew her lips closer to his, leaving only a feather's distance between them. "You took that picture of me and Milo with such love. I didn't realize it at first. Found it in my truck after I'd been gone a couple of weeks. But it nagged at me until I figured it out. You lied. You said you didn't love me, but you lied."

Jillian dipped her head in shame. "I didn't want you to not take your trip because of me."

"I know that now."

"Are you mad?"

"I was." He caressed her neck, teasing her with his swarthy eyes that kept stealing glances at her lips. "But you were right. I needed to go."

"Then why did you come back?"

"I needed to go to realize it was never my trip to take alone. That's not how to honor my brother. You were right. *His* pictures need to be displayed. Shared with other people."

He kissed her then, before she could question anything he just said. His lips moved against her own, and she melted into his embrace. She had been fooling herself if she ever thought she could live without him. Why had it taken her so long to realize this?

"So you're done traveling?"

"For now."

"What about your tent?"

"I have over fifty locations on Paul's list and this great photographer I plan to invite along for the ride." He tucked a wavy lock behind her ear. A twinkle danced in his eyes. "There's plenty of time to use the tent."

$\mathcal{B}$rantley

Three months later . . .

Jillian looked so beautiful, asleep on her pillow with her auburn locks fanned out, Milo nestled into her side. He hated to wake her, but the sunrise was only a few minutes away.

"Jilly," he said, but she didn't stir.

They'd camped out at the spot he had thought about since his brother's passing. Though his Jeep made the trip with little problem, it would have been foolish to attempt such a trek in the dark hours of the morning. They were propped up high in the rooftop tent, Brantley, Jillian, and Milo. The dog had nestled right between them, a big furry wall, wanting to be part of everything during their quick little camping excursion. He didn't seem too fazed at sleeping above ground. Thought lifting him up there was a game.

"Milo," he said, catching the dog's attention. "Time to get up, buddy." He'd have to carry him down the ladder, something that had proven tricky last night, but not impossible. Jillian didn't stir at his words. "You too, Jilly."

Jillian moaned in defense. "Just a few more minutes."

"You're one of those snooze button abusers, aren't you?"

One eye opened, pointed right at him. But she closed it quickly when he caught her. "It's so early, Brantley." Her feet kicked beneath the blanket. After a deep breath, she pushed the covers away and sat up.

"Got to get Milo out. I'll be back."

Jillian assisted with the dog, both down the ladder and back up into the tent when he was finished. They had decided last night that setting up the tripod from inside the rooftop tent might offer the best angle for the sunrise in its full glory.

Once settled back in the tent, he slipped his hand into his pants pocket to ensure the treasure he'd stashed was still there. He'd checked dozens of times since they parked the Jeep last night. His palms were already a little sweaty. What if she said no?

But what if she says yes?

"Need any help?" he asked as he watched Jillian set up the tripod and adjust the camera settings. The first hues of light peeked over the tops of the mountains.

She gave him her cute, appreciative smile. "Not yet."

The last three months had been the best of his life. He didn't need an excuse to stop by the studio, they watched his favorite crime shows nestled on his couch, and Jillian had even gotten him on a standing paddleboard a couple of times.

But was she ready to say yes to spending the rest of their lives together?

"We've got a few minutes yet before it'll be prime picture time." Camera affixed to the tripod and pointed at the perfect angle, Jillian relaxed. The rooftop tent was a little crowded, but he didn't mind. It gave him an excuse to sit closer to Jillian. He put his arm around her shoulder and drew her against him.

"Ever think you'd get Milo in one of these?" he asked, because his nerves would get the best of him if he didn't keep the conversation going.

Milo perked his head at the mention of his name, waiting for either a treat or a head scratch. He settled for the head scratch, as all pizza had been consumed the evening before. They'd used it as bribery when he wasn't too crazy about being lifted into the tent.

"No." Jillian nestled into him closer. "If we

didn't have his P-I-Z-Z-A, I doubt we would've pulled it off."

This felt like home, him sitting with his arm around her, the dog shoving his nose under an arm demanding attention. The sun was getting closer to making its debut for the day, but not quite ready.

"Jilly, I love you. You know that, right?"

"Of course I do. I love you, too, Brantley."

"I've loved you since the first day I met you, when you showed up in that stable." He chuckled, remembering the expression on her face when someone handed her a shovel and pointed at a stall. "You were this dream that walked into my life, and I've never been able to shake you. Even when I left for the Army, you were the one I thought about before I closed my eyes at night."

Jillian turned toward him, her hand sliding along his cheek. She drew him in for a long kiss. Pulling away left him a little dizzy. His hand slipped into his pocket again, this time retrieving the ring before he lost his nerve.

"I can't imagine my life without you in it." He held out the diamond, and Jillian gasped. "Say you'll marry me? Make me the happiest man there is, Jilly."

Tears welled in her eyes, her hands covering half her face. His heart thudded against his ribs as he anxiously awaited her answer.

"I know it might feel fast to you," he continued, "but I've had this ring for over two years. That's how sure I've been that we were meant to be together. I've known it since I first saw you."

"I think some part of me always knew that, but until that crazy week with my dad and Stella, I never realized it. Of course I'll marry you. I love you, Brantley West."

His hands shook as he slipped the ring on her finger, afraid she might change her mind. Afraid he might wake up from a dream. He drew her in for a kiss, taking his time. Her hands wrapped around the back of his neck. They lost themselves for a few moments until Milo let out a bark.

"I think it's time." Jillian nodded toward the front of the tent. She leaned in toward the camera and started snapping shots.

He watched her technique with growing adoration. They'd hang this shot on the living room wall, and he'd proudly tell everyone exactly when his future wife captured this amazing moment in time. "I was thinking Cancun for the wedding."

"What?" Jillian spun away from the camera, her eyes wide.

"Just kidding." He kissed her again before he let her return to taking more photos. "We can get married wherever you want."

~THE END~

Other books in the Starlight Cowboys series:

Cowboys & Starlight (Book 1)

Cowboys & Firelight (Book 2)

Cowboys & Moonlight (Book 4)

N L

Sign up for Jacqueline Winter's newsletter to receive
alerts about current projects and new releases!

http://eepurl.com/du1 8iz

ACKNOWLEDGMENTS

To Nikki - I don't know where I'd be in my writing journey if I'd never sat down at that table years ago. I'm thankful every day that I did.

To my critiquers: Nikki, Mom, Shanon, Becky - Without your feedback, this book would not have turned into the wonderful story that it did. Thank you for your time, your suggestions, and most of all your enthusiasm!

To my editorial and production team: EJ, Brenda, Michelle, Victorine - I'm one lucky author to have such an amazing team behind me with each book. I'm thankful to have found each of you!

To Andy - Thank you for that extra push to get this book finished. Your nudging helped more than you know. Thank you most of all for believing in me.

ABOUT THE AUTHOR

Jacqueline Winters has been writing since she was nine when she'd sneak stacks of paper from her grandma's closet and fill them with adventure. She grew up in small-town Nebraska and spent a decade living in beautiful Alaska. She writes sweet contemporary romance and contemporary romantic suspense.

She's a sucker for happily ever after's, has a sweet tooth that can be sated with cupcakes, and believes sangria was possibly the best invention ever. On a relaxing evening, you can find her at her computer writing her next novel with her faithful dog poking his adorable head out from beneath her desk.

facebook.com/JacquelineWintersRomance

goodreads.com/jacquelinewinters